Deadly Revenge

"Maybe you don't remember me. It's been a hell of a long time since you seen me, but I sure ain't forgot you."

Longarm's eyes had adjusted to the light by now. He looked at Tester's bearded face, its lips drawn into an ugly twist, his eyes glowing hatred. The outlaw's nose was twisted by a long-healed scar where it had once been smashed by Longarm's bullet in the final shootout with the payroll robbers.

"Oh, I recall you real well," Longarm replied levelly. "I put you away once. I'll likely do it again, too, before this is finished up."

"Like hell you will!" Tester growled. He poked the barrel of his revolver into Longarm's stomach. "I'm in charge now, Long. Your hand's played out! I'm gonna enjoy cutting you into little pieces and watching you hurt a lot before you die!"

→•← **TABOR EVANS** →•←

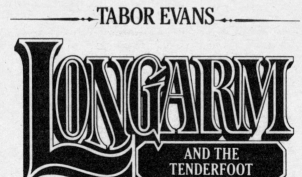

LONGARM

AND THE TENDERFOOT

JOVE BOOKS, NEW YORK

LONGARM AND THE TENDERFOOT

A Jove Book / published by arrangement with
the author

PRINTING HISTORY
Jove edition / November 1985
Second printing / January 1987

ISBN: 0-515-09288-6

Jove Books are published by The Berkley Publishing Group,
200 Madison Avenue, New York, NY 10016.
The words "JOVE BOOKS" and the "J" logo
are trademarks belonging to Jove Publications, Inc.

PRINTED IN THE UNITED STATES OF AMERICA

Chapter 1

Subdued gray light instead of the usual brilliant sunrise gold trickling around the frayed edges of the window shades into his room met Longarm's eyes when they snapped open. As always, he was fully alert the moment he woke up, but this morning his room was darker than usual and his first thought was that it was earlier than his habitual waking time.

Focusing his eyes on the strips of brightness that outlined the tattered edges of the window shade, Longarm saw beads of moisture rolling down the half-inch strip of glass that was visible in the opening. The water combined with the heaviness of the morning air told him what kind of day it was in Denver.

Looks like you brought that damn rain back with you from the Indian Nation, old son, he told himself silently. *Except down there it was wet and hot at the same time, and up here it's bound to be wet and cold.*

Instead of bouncing out of bed with his customary vigor, Longarm lay propped up on his elbow for a moment, studying the room in the grizzly-gray gloom. He looked at the faded wallpaper, the line of hooks set high in the wall between the door and the bed on which his spare clothing hung. As though he was seeing them for the first time, he peered through the gloom, examining the room's spartan furnishings: two chairs, a small table, and a scarred-up oak-veneered bureau. The bureau stood between the twin windows and on it sat a bottle of Tom Moore.

On any other morning, Longarm would have bounced out of bed as soon as he woke up and stepped over to the bureau for his eye-opener, but somehow the amber Maryland rye whiskey lacked its usual appeal without a ray of sunshine seeping through the gap around the tattered shades to give it sparkle. This morning, the gray light and the drops of rain trickling down the windowpanes had brought a depressing chill to the room.

Reaching for his vest, which was draped in its accustomed place over the back of the chair at his bedside, Longarm pushed aside the holstered Colt that hung over the vest and snaked out a long, thin cigar. He picked up one of the matches that lay in a heap on the chair seat, rasped a steel-hard thumbnail across the match-head, and puffed the cheroot alight.

After a few minutes, the acrid smoke that he inhaled somehow made the morning's prospects seem a bit less dismal. Longarm waited until a good half-inch of gray ash had grown on the tip of the cigar. Then he threw aside the blanket that covered him and took the two steps necessary to reach the bureau.

A healthy swallow of the pungent rye whiskey failed to make the day any brighter, but the liquor warmed Longarm's empty stomach and made the morning's prospects seem a bit less dismal. The four-day beard on his face was itching in the damp air and he poured water from the pitcher into his washbowl and splashed the cold liquid on his face until the itching stopped.

Though he needed no confirmation of the weather, Longarm pulled the tattered edge of the window shade aside and peered out into the rain-filled air. It was a slow rain, not hard, just a steady falling of tiny drops from the dull gray clouds that hung low over the mile-high city.

Well, old son, since there ain't a thing you can do to change the damn weather, you might as well get along with it, he told himself. *It don't look all that bad outside, and maybe it'll clear up before the day's out.*

After taking another swallow of Tom Moore, Longarm dressed with his usual speed and efficiency in fresh longjohns taken from the bureau drawer and one of the new gray flannel shirts he'd bought recently and left behind when he started for the Indian Nation on the case he'd just closed. Then he pulled on a pair of dun-colored covert-cloth britches that hugged the calves of his legs almost like a second skin, and a clean pair of socks.

During the few minutes required for him to finish dressing,

2

Longarm glanced at the window from time to time, but the gray day showed no signs of brightening. When at last he'd stomped into his stovepipe cavalry boots, Longarm raised the shades and stood for a moment staring through the drizzle at the shade-blinded windows of the house next door. Still reluctant to go outside in spite of his stomach's message that breakfast time had arrived, he delayed his departure still further by dragging his saddlebags to the bed and sitting down to put the tools of his trade in order.

Longarm's .44-.40 Colt double-action revolver received his attention first. The cheroot he'd lighted was little more than a stub by now, and he tossed it into the spittoon that stood by the bureau before sliding the weapon from its well-worn open-toed holster. Although the gun had come from Colt's New Haven factory only a few years earlier, the gunsmiths who had produced it would barely have recognized it, in spite of the Colt name and rearing mustang trademark at the top of its grips.

Not only had the lanyard ring been removed from the pistol's butt; the high half-moon front sight had been filed down to a tiny hump that would not drag on the holster when the weapon was whipped out in a fast draw. However, the most radical change was invisible: the barrel had been shortened by half an inch, and it and the cylinder rebored from its original .41 caliber to handle the heavier and more potently lethal .44-.40 cartridges.

Flipping the loading port open, Longarm ejected the five cartridges in the cylinder. He'd reloaded hurriedly after his fracas with Cade on the train the previous day, and he hadn't given the three fresh loads his usual close attention when he replaced the spent rounds.

He found the shells in satisfactory condition, but while the gun was unloaded he took a stubby cleaning rod from his saddlebags and ran it down the barrel. Returning the shells to the cylinder, he slid the Colt back into its holster and buckled on his gunbelt. Shrugging into his vest, Longarm picked up his watch and the double-barreled derringer attached to it by the chain, and dropped the watch in his lower left-hand vest pocket, the derringer in the right. The derringer needed no attention; Longarm had not fired it recently.

3

Mindful of the drizzling rain, he stepped to the wall hook beside the door and donned his long coat before settling his tobacco-brown hat squarely on his head and starting out the door.

On the porch of the rooming house he paused to light a fresh cheroot and to peer distastefully at the dismal sky. The drizzle he had seen from his window upstairs was now almost a full-fledged rain. Rivulets of water were drooling down the peeling gray paint of the walls on each side of the porch, and the boards of the walk that led to the gravelled street held small puddles in their cupped warps. Hunching his shoulders, Longarm walked a bit faster than usual to the cindered pathway and started toward the Cherry Creek bridge.

By the time he'd reached Colfax Avenue and started toward downtown Denver, the drizzle had fulfilled its promise and turned into a slow, steady rain. Ahead, the capitol building's dome was barely visible. A light showed in George Masters's barbership, and though his stomach was reminding him it was breakfast time, Longarm went into the shop.

"Looks to me like you got out of bed on the wrong side this morning," Masters greeted him. "And from the way your face looks, you've spent a week or so someplace where there aren't any barbershops handy."

"I had to make a quick run to Indian Territory," Longarm said. "And I'll give you a dollar to a plugged dime for every barbershop you'll find in them tanglewoods that starts about halfway down to the Canadian River."

"A hard case?"

"Not so's you'd notice. I closed it all right," Longarm replied, hanging his coat on the clothes tree and dropping his hat on the same hook. "Look at what it's like outside. You know I just ain't all that fond of rain, George."

"Well, cheer up," Masters replied. "Give it another month or so and it'll turn to snow."

"And I like snow a lot less'n I do rain," Longarm said. He settled into the barber chair and raised his chin to let Masters drape the cloth around him.

"Then I don't guess there's much I can do to help you," the barber told him. "Except get rid of those pinfeathers on your

4

jaws and trim your hair so you'll look presentable again."

"Get on with it, then," Longarm said, leaning back and closing his eyes. "And if that razor of yours ain't dull, the way it is sometimes, I might just as well finish out my sleep."

Three-quarters of an hour later, his spirit refreshed by the shave and his customary breakfast of ham and eggs and fried potatoes at Sam Chee's restaurant on Cherokee Street, Longarm reached the federal building. He mounted the marble stairs to the second floor. The door to the Denver district office of the U. S. Marshal was just swinging closed when Longarm reached it. He pushed through before it closed completely and saw the young pink-cheeked clerk pulling out the chair at his desk.

"Deputy Long!" the young man exclaimed. "I didn't expect to see you here at this time of day!"

"Any reason why not?" Longarm asked. "Far as I know, I still work here."

"Oh, of course! I just mean . . . well, it's so early. . . ."

"Never mind," Longarm said, going past the clerk into Billy Vail's office.

A light from inside shone through the door's frosted glass upper panel. Longarm opened the door and entered without knocking. Vail looked up from his paper-piled desk and when he saw Longarm his eyes widened, and he turned to look at the big Vienna Regulator clock that stood on a wall shelf across the room. For a moment, the chief marshal stared at the clock, then turned back to Longarm.

"What's wrong with you this morning?" Vail asked.

"Not a thing, as far as I know," Longarm replied. "What makes you think there is, Billy?"

Vail nodded toward the clock and said, "There's bound to be something wrong, or you wouldn't be showing up on time. I'll have to put a ring around today on my calendar."

"Now, that's enough funning, Billy," Longarm said. "I got back too late to check in last night, and figured I better get on down here a mite early."

"I suppose you closed your case, or you wouldn't be back," Vail observed. "And if I know you, I'll wait a month for your report, so you'd better sit down and tell me about it."

Longarm pulled the red morocco upholstered chair he fa-

5

vored up to Vail's desk. Settling into the chair, he pulled a fresh cigar from his pocket and fished in his vest for matches.

"There ain't a lot to report, Billy," he said. "Just like we figured, Cade made a beeline for the Indian Territory."

"And I assume you caught up with him before he got to a safe hideout, or you'd still be looking for him."

"Something like that." Longarm nodded. "He headed south, along the North Fork of the Canadian. I'd imagine he figured he'd get to the main river and hole up in the brakes."

"Obviously he didn't get to the thickets before you caught up with him, or you'd still be down there."

"Well, Cade didn't think very good, Billy. That shot the mail clerk got off before he died tore up Cade's ear pretty bad, and he put a bandage on it. A lot of folks that wouldn't't've paid no attention to him otherwise noticed that bandage. It wasn't such a much of a job to follow him."

"You delivered Cade to the jail when you got in last night, I suppose?"

"Well, no. Not exactly."

"Maybe you'd better tell me what 'not exactly' means," the chief marshal suggested. "You did catch up with Cade and arrest him, I suppose?"

"Oh, sure. Like I said a minute ago, he'd left a trail even a tenderfoot could follow without no trouble."

When Longarm stopped to relight his cheroot and didn't continue his report at once, Vail reminded him, "You still haven't explained what 'not exactly' means."

Through a cloud of blue smoke, Longarm went on, "Well, I had my rifle, and all Cade had was his pistol. He seen right away that he was outranged, so he put up his hands after I'd let off a couple of rounds. I took him up to the Wichita spur and got on the Santa Fe. Had him handcuffed, of course, and fastened one of the cuffs to the seat arm, just like regulations say. He acted right good till we stopped at Hays."

"Well, I'm glad you didn't have any trouble," Vail commented when Longarm stopped to inhale again.

"Now, I didn't say there wasn't no trouble, Billy. Matter of fact, there was a mite of a dustup. You see, the railroad butcher boy come on board the train at Hays, and Cade said he was

6

hungry. I got him a sandwich and took the handcuff off the chair seat so he could eat it. Then before I could stop him, the son of a bitch jumped out the window."

"Which I guess you'd opened because he told you he needed some fresh air?" Vail asked.

"Now, you know me better'n that, Billy," Longarm replied. "The window was closed, but Cade dived right through the glass. Thing is, he'd seen the conductor standing outside by the car on the station platform, and I guess he must've remembered that a train conductor generally carries a gun."

Vail broke in to say, "I don't think you need to finish, but go ahead anyhow."

"Oh, I had to shoot him, of course," Longarm said. "There wasn't much else I could do. He'd already let off a shot at me before I drew and got to the window. He ducked under the train then, and I had to jump out the window so's I could get a bead on him. I pinned him down behind the wheel trucks and when he leaned out to draw a bead on me, I shot first."

Longarm stopped to puff his cheroot.

"Is that all?" Vail asked.

"Well, Cade was about as dead as a man can be," Longarm replied. "I didn't see what I could do except bring his body on here to Denver. It's wrapped up in a blanket down at the freight depot, so you can tell the young fellow out in the office to fix up with the undertaker about burying him."

Vail sat silently for a moment, then nodded slowly. "It sounds like you did what you had to do," he said. "Just be sure to get all the details in your report."

"Sure, Billy. And when you come right down to it, I guess I saved the government a lot of money, now that Cade ain't going to stand trial for killing that Indian agent down on the Cheyenne Reservation. It wouldn't've been a real open and shut case, and he might've got off free. You know that."

"I suppose," Vail replied. "But it'll mean more paperwork for me, and I've got about as much as I need right now." He waved at the stacks of documents piled atop his desk, then went on, "Old Judge Cassidy's due to take the bench at the court term that starts next week, and you know how he is. He expects full panels and wants everything done by the book."

7

"You mean I'm going to be serving subpoenas on witnesses and rounding up jury panels for a while, Billy?"

"It looks that way. And courtroom duty, too. You're the only deputy I've got right now; everybody else is out of town on other jobs."

"Well, I can't say I'm sorry," Longarm said thoughtfully. "I ain't had local duty for a spell. It'll be a nice change. I sorta miss the bunch down at the Windsor, and I can't recall how long it's been since I sat in on a game with 'em."

"If I ever get this desk of mine clear, I might even sit in myself an evening or two," Vail told him. "Well, write up your report and give it to the clerk. Then you might as well take the rest of the day off."

Longarm's jaw dropped when he heard his chief's unusual suggestion. "You mean it, Billy? What about all them papers we got to get ready for Judge Cassidy?"

"That paperwork's going to have to wait," the chief marshal replied. "If you haven't looked at a calendar, this is the day for my telegraph conference with the big boys in Washington."

"Now, you know I ain't around the office enough to keep up with things like that. Is something special happening?"

"Not that I know of," Vail said. "Most of what I get on those two-way wire conferences could just as well be handled by mail. But once in a while they turn out to be worth the half-day they eat up, and since I don't have any way of knowing in advance what'll come out of them, I've got to keep to the schedule."

"Which means you'll be setting down in the basement in the telegraph room swapping words back and forth with some deputy attorney general back East."

"That's about the size of it," Vail agreed. "But it's part of my job, so I'd better get on downstairs and attend to it."

Longarm walked with his chief through the outer office and down the stairs to the first floor. They parted with a wave, Vail continuing to the basement where the telegraph room with its direct wire to Washington was located, and Longarm walked on out the door to Colfax Avenue. The skies were still gray, but the rain had diminished to a drizzle. He stood on the sidewalk for a moment, faced with the unaccustomed luxury of having an entire day that he could spend as he chose.

Old son, he told himself, *about the smartest thing you can do is hyper on back to your room and crawl into bed. There ain't a thing you got to do, nobody to chase after and nobody chasing after you, and this weather ain't fit to be out in. You can catch up on some of the sleep you lost without having to keep one eye open in case a crook's trying to sneak up on you, and rest up for that poker game tonight.*

Chapter 2

In the little room off the Windsor Hotel bar, the smoke of half a dozen cigars hung over the round poker table in a thick blue haze. Longarm waited for the fifth card to fall on the four of the new hand that lay on the green felt in front of him. The card dropped and he picked up the hand. Around the table, the five other players were doing the same thing.

Fanning out his cards, Longarm glanced at them. He saw the deuce and eight of clubs, the four of hearts, ten of spades, and jack of diamonds. It was typical of the hands he'd held all evening. No two cards offered any possibility of being combined into a winning hand. Keeping his face expressionless, Longarm laid the cards face down on the felt. The dealer, Joe Torrington, was on his left, and he knew there was plenty of time left before he had to make a decision to stay in or fold.

"It's your ante, Billy," Torrington told Vail.

"I'll let you boys in for a dollar this time," Vail said, and tossed a red chip in the center of the table. "And since I've had a busy day and tomorrow's going to be another one just like it, I'll give you notice that I've got to pull out after this hand."

"Cheap enough," Ed Hopkins nodded, adding his chip to Vail's. "And I'd better quit after this hand, too."

"If we're all quitting, let's make it a good pot, then," Dan Cassidy said. "I'll double the ante." He added two red chips to the pair on the table and looked around expectantly.

"What I've got's not worth it," Paul Sanders commented. "But I'll be a sport and ride with you." He added a pair of reds to the pot.

Throughout the evening, Longarm had held only indifferent hands. He'd won a couple of small pots, but was still almost ten dollars in the hole. Even before Vail had spoken, he'd made up his mind to play one final hand. Now, without waiting for Torrington to prompt him, he dropped his ante on the table.

"You're keeping it too cheap," Torrington said. "I'll boost the ante another dollar." He added to the pot, waited until the other players brought their bets up, and picked up the shrunken deck, saying, "All right, boys. Cards?"

"Give me two good ones, Joe," Billy Vail said. He tossed his discards on the table and added the newly dealt cards to the three he'd kept.

"Just one for me," Ed Hopkins announced. He followed Vail in adding to the discards after he'd picked up the new card Torrington dropped in front of him.

"I'll play what I've got," Dan Cassidy announced.

"Well, now!" Torrington said. "Looks like we better be careful from here on out." He asked the next man, "Are you staying in, Paul?"

"Sure. And I need two," Paul Sanders replied, adding to the discard pile and picking up the cards he'd been dealt.

"How about you?" Torrington asked Longarm.

While watching the draw, Longarm had made up his mind. He tossed all five of his cards on the discard stack and added a red chip to the pot as he said, "I'm in, but what I got ain't good enough to draw to. I'll just pay my dollar and get a new hand."

Torrington fanned out the few cards remaining from the draw and said, "I'm playing what I got in the deal, so there's just enough here to oblige you, Long." He put the five cards in front of Longarm, who picked them up, then turned to Cassidy. "You kicked up the ante, Dan. It's your say-so."

"Five bucks," Cassidy announced as he flipped a white chip into the pot.

"That's cheap enough to keep me in," Sanders said, following Cassidy's example.

Longarm looked at his cards for the first time. He saw they were all black, then a second look showed him that they were all spades running in sequence from the eight to the queen. He put a white chip in and said casually, "Guess I'll go along for the ride, too."

"It'll cost you more than that," Torrington told Longarm.

He shoved two white chips across the table. "I'm raising."

"I don't want to be the first one to fold," Vail remarked casually, tossing his chips in.

"And I feel like Billy does," Hopkins said. "I'm in, too."

"I'll meet Billy's raise and boost it five," Cassidy said quickly, adding a blue chip to the growing pot.

Vail and Hopkins silently added another white chip apiece, and Cassidy turned to Sanders to ask, "You staying, Paul?"

"For now, I am," Sanders replied, pushing in a blue chip.

Cassidy added a white chip without speaking and Longarm did the same. Torrington frowned and studied his cards a moment.

"I'm not going to let a good pot die." he said, tossing two blue chips on the pile that was accumulating in the center of the table. "What d'you say to that, Billy?"

"About all I can say is that I'll stay with you for this round, anyhow," Vail said, tossing in a blue.

"I've got to go along for now," Ed Hopkins said, frowning. He pushed in his bet and turned to Cassidy. "You going to raise again, Dan?"

"You just better be ready to kick in another ten if you want to see my cards," Cassidy smiled, tossing two more blue chips on the heap. "This is where the boys drop out and the men keep on going."

Sanders and Longarm met the raise silently again, but Torrington said, "Hell, if the game's about to break up, let's make it a real pot. How does another twenty on top of your raise strike you men?"

"It sounds damned expensive, but I'll see it," Vail said.

"I think Joe's bluffing," Hopkins said unexpectedly. He picked up four blue chips and let them fall on top of the heap already in the center of the table. "I'm going to smoke you out, Joe. Your twenty and twenty more."

Longarm glanced down at his stack of chips. He had enough to meet Hopkins's raise, but not enough to stand another boost, and he was sure that both Cassidy and Torrington would raise. He waited until Cassidy had raised the bet another ten dollars and Sanders had met the boost, then said, "I aim to stay in, men, but if I do, I'll have to play the pot short."

"You're good for it," Torrington told him quickly, looking around at the other players. "Anybody object?"

None of them did. Longarm shoved his last chips into the pot and waited, sure that Torrington would raise. When the boost of twenty dollars came as he'd expected, Longarm took two blue chips out of the pot, and two more when Cassidy raised it another twenty.

Including the forty dollars owed the winner by Longarm, there was now more than five hundred dollars in the pot, a sizeable sum compared to the usual betting in the long-standing game. He was sure the pot would not grow much larger, and his hunch proved correct when Cassidy called after Torrington's next raise.

"Lay 'em down, then," Torrington said. "I'd like to see what's got you so reckless, Dan."

Cassidy spread his cards, a diamond flush from the deuce to the six. "Go on, Joe," he challenged. "Can you top it?"

Torrington shook his head and spread his hand, three sevens and a pair of queens.

Vail said, "I thought I was doing good to hold four treys."

Sanders shrugged and laid his cards face down on the table. Hopkins and Vail shook their heads. Cassidy was reaching for the pile of chips when Longarm spoke.

"You got a right pretty hand there, Dan," he said quietly, laying his cards face up on the table. "But I got one that's prettier. My straight flush runs up to the lady. Looks like that pot belongs to me."

For a moment, Cassidy stared unbelievingly at Longarm's cards. Then he grinned wryly and shoved the pile of chips over to Longarm. He said, "You took us all in, Long, sitting there letting us do all the work."

"That's what I call good poker," Torrington put in. "We'll know to watch him closer from here on."

"It ain't hard to sit tight when you're pretty sure you got the cards," Longarm said quietly. "But I'll tell you what I'll do. You boys come out losers, so I'll pick up the bill at the bar."

"You cut yourself a right fat hog there," Billy Vail told Longarm as they left the Windsor and started walking down Larimer toward the square.

Even at this late hour of the night, there were still a few hackney cabs and private carriages on Larimer Street. After falling steadily until late in the day, the rain had stopped now and there was a sharp nip in the air. Longarm and Vail were the last of the poker players to leave the hotel; the chief marshal had stopped with Longarm in the bar while the bill for the group's drinks was settled.

Vail went on, "There must've been something like five hundred in that pot. It's the biggest one I remember we've had since this bunch started playing regularly."

"I don't mind telling you, it's one of the biggest pots I ever hauled in since I begun playing poker," Longarm replied. "But I just lucked out, getting that pat hand in the draw."

"We'll all be laying for you at our next session," Vail warned. Then he shook his head and went on, "Except that I doubt you'll make the next game or two."

"Now, hold on, Billy!" Longarm remonstrated. "If I catch on to what you're getting at, you got a case for me to go out on right away."

"I'm afraid you're right," Vail nodded.

"I ain't even had a chance to send out my laundry yet!" Longarm said. "How soon do I have to leave?"

"Why don't we wait and talk about it tomorrow," Vail suggested as they neared Sixteenth Street. "I haven't had a chance to look over the material I got on the wire from Washington today."

"Sounds like it's another one of them mixed-up businesses that winds up with me not knowing who I'm after," Longarm told his chief. "But I guess it'll hold over."

"I guess it'll have to," Vail replied. "This is my corner. I'll see you in the office, first thing in the morning."

Longarm nodded and continued walking alone down Larimer. He was just outside the fringe of Denver's "lowers" now, the area that extended several blocks along Market Street and spilled over into the intersection streets for a block or so. A passing hackney cab rumbling down the street caught Longarm's eye when it stopped at the corner ahead, a few yards past the swinging door of a saloon.

Remembering his unexpectedly full pockets, Longarm decided that he'd hire the hack and ride home in style. He reached the saloon and pushed through the batwings. Two men at the bar with steins of beer in front of them and the aproned barkeep were its only occupants. One of the beer drinkers wore a long-billed cloth cap and the other had on a brown derby hat. Longarm picked the man with the cap as the cabby and stopped in front of him.

"I'd guess that's your hack out in front?" he asked.

"It sure is, mister," the man replied. "But if you want to hire it, you'll have to wait till I finish my beer."

Longarm glanced at the man's stein, saw it was half empty, and nodded. "Go ahead," he said. Then, as he looked at the backbar and saw a bottle of Tom Moore, he decided not to wait until he was back in his room for a nightcap.

"I'll have a tot of that Maryland rye while I'm waiting for the hack," he told the barkeep.

Even though he had a fare waiting, the hackman showed no inclination to hurry. He sipped his beer slowly while the other beer drinker emptied his stein and left. Longarm swallowed half his shot of whiskey in one gulp and lighted a cheroot.

At last the cabby tilted his stein far back to take a last swallow, and Longarm tossed off what was left of his rye. He and the hackman started for the door at the same time. Longarm stepped aside to let the cab driver reach the darkened street first, then followed him through the batwings.

When the hackie opened the door of his cab, Longarm put a foot in the stirrup-step to hoist himself inside. He was bending forward to clear the top of the hack's door, suspended between the brick sidewalk and the carriage, when the hackman suddenly swivelled away from the door. He got a shoulder under Longarm's buttocks and half-lifted, half-pushed him inside.

Longarm felt himself being shoved up and ahead. He brought up his arms instinctively as he fell forward in an awkward sprawl. His hands met a pair of trousered legs and at the same time he felt the unmistakable pressure of a revolver's cold steel muzzle dig into his neck at the point of his jawbone.

"You just stay on the floor and lay still if you want to keep on living," a man's voice gritted from the darkness. "This gun's cocked, and it's got a hair trigger. One move outa you and I'll pull it."

Longarm did not reply, but he did not move, either. He felt the hack driver's hands close on his booted ankles and shove his long legs inside. Then he heard the door slammed shut. The carriage shook as the driver mounted to the outside seat. Then Longarm felt a swaying as the hackney moved ahead.

"Keep your hands right where they are," the voice of the man in the seat warned. Longarm racked his brain, but he did not recognize the voice as being that of any lawbreaker he'd encountered before. His captor went on, "I'm going to reach down and get your pistol. If you're smart as you're made out to be, you'll stay real still while I'm doing it, because I still got my finger on the trigger of my own gun."

Longarm felt a hand move down in the narrow space between his side and the seat, grope for the butt of his Colt, and draw the revolver from its holster. He kept silent and remained motionless while the man in the seat lifted the gun away. Even then, the man kept the muzzle of his own weapon pressed to Longarm's neck while the hackney cab rumbled over the brick pavement to its unknown destination.

Soon the brick gave way to gravel and the gravel to dirt. After what seemed to be a very long time to Longarm in his uncomfortable position, the cab creaked to a halt. He felt the hackney sway as the driver swung to the ground, then the rush of cool night air as the door opened.

"I got him covered now, Brice," the hackman said. "Let's get him inside. Tester's going to be right glad to see him."

"All right, Long," the man addressed as Brice said, taking his gun away from Longarm's neck for the first time. "You heard him. Back out real slow."

Longarm began backing out of the cab, but said nothing. His mind was busy calling up the memory of the name mentioned by the hackie. He remembered Tester only vaguely as an outlaw he'd arrested years before, in Wyoming Territory, the leader of a gang that had ambushed and robbed an army payroll wagon on its way to Fort Washakie in the Shoshone country.

Tester had escaped hanging and drawn a fifty-year sentence in federal prison because his lawyer picked a loophole in the evidence and convinced a jury that no proof had been offered that Tester had fired any of the shots which killed two members of the wagon's escort. Longarm's thinking was interrupted by the hackman's gun prodding into his back.

"March along inside now," Brice ordered as he dropped from the cab to stand beside Longarm. "The man that sent us out to pick you up has been waiting a long time to see you."

With the muzzle of a gun pressing firmly into his spine, Longarm had little choice. He followed Brice up the steps to the porch. The door of the house opened, the glow of a lamp inside backlighting the figure of the man who stood in the doorway. He stepped aside as Longarm followed Brice through the door, then closed it when the cabby was inside. He stepped around to face Longarm.

"Maybe you don't remember me," he snarled. "It's been a hell of a long time since you seen me, but I sure ain't forgot you! Hell, me and the boys here's been watching you all day, ever since Rafe spotted you getting off the train last night."

Longarm had recognized his captor at once. He said coolly, "I figured you'd still be in the pen, Tester. Seems to me you drawed a fifty-year term for that job I brought you in for."

"Well, I got out and now I found you, and that's enough," Tester snarled. "I been figuring all them years I was in that stinking pen how I'd even up the score, and now it's my turn!"

Longarm's eyes had adjusted to the light by now. He looked at Tester's bearded face, its lips drawn into an ugly twist, his eyes glowing hatred. The outlaw's nose was twisted by a long-healed scar where it had once been smashed by Longarm's bullet in the final shootout with the payroll robbers.

"Oh, I recall you real well," Longarm replied levelly, stalling for time while he took stock of his new situation. "And I ain't forgot them two soldiers you backshot when you jumped that Army pay wagon. Sure, I put you away, Tester. I'll likely do it again, too, before this is finished up."

"Like hell you will!" Tester growled. "I'm in charge now,

17

Long. Your hand's played out. I'm gonna enjoy cutting you into little pieces and watching you hurt a lot before you die!"

Longarm did not bother to answer the outlaw's threats. His eyes were flicking over the room, looking for anything that might help him break free. The place had little furniture, only three or four straight chairs and a table on which stood the coal-oil lamp that lighted the room.

"Rafe, you and Brice tie him up in one of them chairs," Tester ordered, without taking his eyes off Longarm. He poked the barrel of his revolver into Longarm's stomach. "Start backing up, Long. I'll feel better when you're tied so tight you can't move. I ain't forgot what a slippery son of a bitch you are."

Longarm knew his only chance was to play for time. He took a backward step toward the chair. For a moment his move relieved the pressure of Tester's revolver muzzle in his stomach, but the outlaw was taking no chances. He shoved his pistol forward as Longarm moved.

Without taking his eyes off Longarm, Tester asked Brice, "I guess you got his gun first off, didn't you?"

"Don't worry," Brice replied. "I took it off him myself the minute we had him in the hack."

"Did you search him all over?" Tester asked. "He might be toting a backup."

"Now, how in hell could I search him, cramped up in that cab?" Brice asked.

"Better look now, then," Tester said. "Before you tie him in the chair."

Longarm had been busy sorting out possibilities during the brief exchange between Tester and Brice. He knew that as long as he was forced to keep his arms in the air, Tester's bullet would cut him down before he could reach his derringer. Longarm had no intention of losing the one ace that he held in the hole, though he still hadn't solved the problem of cutting down all three of his captors with the two shots the derringer would give him. As he and Tester got within arm's length of the table, Brice came up to carry out his search and Tester took a half step aside to let his hireling reach Longarm more easily.

Longarm twisted his body, a move he'd planned in the split

second after he had heard Tester's command. It was a move he was gambling on to draw Brice's attention to the pockets of his coat. Brice took the gambit. He plunged his hand into Longarm's right-hand coat pocket, and his groping hand encountered the loose gold coins of Longarm's winnings at the poker game.

"Damned if he ain't just loaded down with cash!" Brice exclaimed, pawing in the pocket. He laid his revolver on the table and began scooping out gold pieces. "Look at this!" he said to Tester. "The son of a bitch must've robbed somebody to get this much money! And it's all in gold, too!"

Avarice showing in his tone, Tester commanded, "Well, go on and get all of it out!"

Brice returned to his exploration of Longarm's coat pocket. He dug out another handful of gold pieces and added them to the loose heap on the table, then turned back to Longarm for a final exploration of the pocket. Longarm risked turning his head far enough around to watch the other two men. Rafe, the hackman, was moving toward the table, and Tester had shifted his position to see the gold more clearly. Brice's revolver lay beside the glowing pile of gold.

Longarm knew his moment had come. He lunged back, bumping into Brice and throwing him off balance. At the same time, he dropped his arms. He reached for Brice's pistol with one hand and at the same time yanked at his watch-chain with his other hand to pull the derringer from his vest pocket.

He got a grip on the derringer before his groping hand found the butt of the revolver on the table, and his first shot from the stubby little pistol caught Tester in the chest. The outlaw staggered back under the impact of the heavy slug. Tester got off a wild shot as he was falling, but the bullet tore into the ceiling.

Within a split second Longarm had swivelled the derringer's short barrel to cut down Rafe before the cabby could raise his own gun. By now, Longarm had Brice's pistol in his free hand. He jammed its muzzle into Brice's chest and fired. The impact of the slug sent Brice staggering backward. He stayed on his feet for a moment, his body swaying, then crumpled into a heap on the floor.

Lead from Tester's revolver whistled past Longarm's head.

Longarm swivelled his weapon and fired. His bullet went true and Tester's gun fell from a lifeless hand.

Slowly, Longarm lowered the revolver and his derringer. He looked at the sprawled figures of the three outlaws and shook his head. *Well, old son,* he told himself, *you come outa this one better'n you had a right to. And them three renegades sure ain't going to bother nobody any more!*

Chapter 3

"Well, damn it, Billy!" Longarm protested to the chief marshal. "It ain't my fault them renegades set up that trap and tried to kill me last night!"

"I didn't say it was," Vail replied.

Longarm's indignation was so great that he ignored Vail's placating remark and went on, "You sure wouldn't expect me to let 'em get away with it! When I got caught in that trap them outlaws had set up, the only thing I seen to do was shoot my way out! I'd like to've seen the damn sheriff do any different!"

"If you'll stop and think a minute, you'll remember all I said is that Sheriff Remey is upset," Vail reminded him.

"Don't you think I know what that means, Billy?" Longarm demanded. "That old buzzard jumps on me every time I clear out one of the crooks' nests around Denver that it seems like he ain't able to find. This ain't the first time he's run to you with his bellyaching!"

"Now, just cool down!" Vail said. "I'm not blaming you for what happened. I'm just passing on what the sheriff said. He figures you were butting in on his jurisdiction. As far as I'm concerned, Tester was a fugitive who'd escaped from a federal prison, and that made him as much our business as he was Sheriff Remey's. The way I look at it, you did the sheriff a favor."

Under the influence of the chief marshal's sympathetic words, Longarm was beginning to cool down. "That makes me feel some better," he nodded. "I guess I'll just leave you to argue it out with Sheriff Remey. You're handier at jobs like that than I'll ever be."

"Fine. Now, let's forget about last night and talk over that case the deputy attorney general told me to put you on during

21

our telegraph conference yesterday."

"That'd be the one you mentioned when we was leaving the poker game last night?"

Vail nodded, busy sorting through the heap of telegraph flimsies in his hand. He found the one he'd been looking for and said, "The case is over in New Mexico Territory, and Washington has put an 'urgent' tab on it."

"Meaning they're saying frog, and we better hop."

"Something like that," Vail agreed.

"If Washington's all edgy about this case, I figure there's bound to be politics mixed up in it. Am I right or wrong?" Longarm asked.

"You could put it that way," Vail agreed, adding hastily, "But not just politics. Money. A lot of money. Four million dollars, to be exact."

Longarm whistled. Then he frowned as he said, "That's more than all of New Mexico Territory's worth, Billy!"

"It's not exactly New Mexico Territory we're talking about. When I say money, I mean two million dollars in U. S. Treasury bonds and two million dollars' worth of Atlantic & Pacific Railroad bonds are missing, and your job's to find them."

"You mean somebody stole them?"

"If they're missing, I suppose they got stolen," Vail said. "I can't see anybody losing something like that."

"I can understand where the bonds come in," Longarm told Vail. "But what was that you said about politics?"

"Something else is missing, too," the chief marshal replied. "A copy of a grant treaty giving the Atlantic & Pacific Railroad the right to build the only U. S. rail line that'll ever cross the border into Mexico."

"Now you're getting me confused, Billy," Longarm said. "I could keep the SP and the Santa Fe straight, but three railroads is one too many. I guess you just better start out from the beginning and tell me what all else is wound up in this case."

"I wish I could, but the information I've got is pretty scanty. You'll have to find out the details from Chief Marshal Otero when you get to Sante Fe. He's the one who asked for you to be assigned to the case."

22

"Chief Marshal Otero?" Longarm asked, his voice puzzled. "Seems I recall hearing you say he died a little while back."

"That's right, he did," Vail agreed after a moment of thought. "And I don't think I ever heard who was appointed to replace him. For all I know, somebody might be filling the job on a temporary appointment. But that doesn't matter, Long. You'll find out soon enough."

"I'd sure like to know more about this case, Billy. How'd all that much in bonds happen to come up missing?"

Vail studied the telegraph flimsies again for a moment, then said, "It seems the Santa Fe has struck a deal with the Southern Pacific to do a little bit of right-of-way trading. The Santa Fe's had to stop building its tracks west from New Mexico because under that Federal Railroad Act Congress passed a few years ago, there's got to be at least two hundred miles between railroads that run east and west."

"That means they'd have to go north, then," Longarm said thoughtfully. "And they can't do that because it'd put 'em too close to the UP."

"Not exactly," Vail replied. "There's plenty of distance between the SP and the UP to let the Santa Fe build on out west, but if they stick to that two-hundred-mile spacing, the Santa Fe line would have to be built through the Rockies most of the way, then they'd still have the Sierra Nevada to cross when they got close to the West Coast."

"Why, that'd take 'em twenty years and cost more money than I can even imagine!" Longarm said.

"That's what the Santa Fe people figure, too," Vail nodded. "But until a little while ago, they hadn't come up with anything better. That was before old Cyrus Holliday pulled a rabbit out of his hat."

"It must've been a good-sized rabbit," Longarm observed.

"Yes, it is. You see, Long, when Holliday started the Santa Fe, he'd bought up the old Atlantic & Pacific Railroad that went broke a few years before."

"Wasn't that the railroad that had a right-of-way across the Rockies to start out with?" Longarm broke in to ask.

Vail nodded. "Those fool Eastern railroad men didn't know how much they were biting off. They're used to building through

23

little pimple-sized hills like the Appalachians and the Ozarks."

"So the men backing the Atlantic & Pacific threw in the sponge when they found out what the Rockies is like?" Longarm smiled.

"Just as soon as they saw that the Rockies were a lot bigger bite than they could chew. But the A&P had something that the Southern Pacific really wanted, even if Holliday didn't tumble to it when he'd bought 'em up."

"What was that?"

"A few years back, when Diaz first took power in Mexico, he pushed a law through the Mexican Congress that allowed only one foreign railroad to come into the country. The Atlantic & Pacific had just been organized and they jumped in and got the grant to build that one railroad."

"So when the SP and the Santa Fe come along, they found the door'd already been slammed shut?"

"Exactly. The A&P had built a couple of hundred miles of track down from the border along the Mexican coast, mainly to haul ore up from the mines around Durango. I understand they've surveyed all the way to Mexico City, though."

"Then when the Santa Fe bought the A&P, they got the railroad in Mexico, too, I take it?"

"Of course," Vail nodded. "But the Santa Fe doesn't want a railroad in Mexico. They've got their hands full building on out to California."

"They used the Mexican line to get a deal out of the SP?"

"They sure did. From what I understand, Colis Huntington wants that Mexican railroad for the SP real bad. That's why he made the deal he did to let the Santa Fe fudge on that two-hundred-mile separation limit. Well, the deal's been closed, or will be as soon as the Santa Fe delivers four million dollars in cash and bonds and the Mexican grant treaty to the SP."

"That's the same treaty you told me about a minute ago?" Longarm broke in to ask.

"Yep," Vail replied. "The one and only copy was with the bonds that've disappeared. It seems like somebody in the State Department in Washington lost the U. S. copy and the copies in Mexico got destroyed during the fighting between . . . well, take your choice of Huerta or Juarez or Diaz or whoever else pulled off a revolution, or tried to pull off one. All anybody really knows is that the only copy is the one that went to the Atlantic & Pacific Railroad, and the A&P passed it on to the Santa Fe."

"How come that copy of the treaty's so important?" Longarm asked, a puzzled frown wrinkling his forehead. "Everybody knows what's in it, don't they?"

"Pretty much. But it's important because of that law Diaz pushed through the Mexican Congress, the one that allows just one United States railroad to operate in Mexico. Without the copy of the actual treaty to back 'em up, the Santa Fe wouldn't have anything to sell the SP, and the deal would be off."

Longarm shook his head. "You do pick out the damnedest cases for me, Billy!"

"Remember, it wasn't me that picked you out for this one," Vail reminded Longarm. "It was the chief marshal for New Mexico Territory. And he didn't ask me about it. He asked the assistant attorney general in Washington."

"That's a pretty big man, I guess? The one in Washington?"

"I'll put it to you this way," Vail replied. "He's next in line to the attorney general, and the attorney general is next in line to the President. I don't see that you can go much higher."

Longarm sat thoughtfully for a moment. Then he asked Vail, "You know how I feel right this minute, Billy?"

"No. Suppose you tell me."

"Well, up in Montana Territory they was hanging an old outlaw named Zeke Carter. As I recall, it was about the first time there'd been a hanging there, and everybody and his dog turned out to watch it. Somebody asked old Zeke how he felt, being the center of so much attention, and he said if it wasn't for the honor of being the main attraction, he'd resign."

"Now, hold on a minute—" Vail began.

Longarm cut him off. "Don't worry, Billy. I ain't aiming to quit on you. I'll catch the evening train south."

"That's better," Vail nodded. "Now, the clerk's got all your travel papers and expense vouchers ready. And I'd say the place for you to start is in Santa Fe. The chief marshal of the Territory can sure tell you more about the case than I can."

• • •

For Longarm, the trip to Santa Fe had meant retracing an old familiar route. He'd taken the Denver & Rio Grande out of Denver to Raton, transferred there to the Santa Fe. The summer rush of tourists had slacked off with the approach of summer's end, and he'd been the only passenger who alighted at Lamy and rode the creaking stage to Santa Fe.

When the stage pulled up at the stables of La Fonda Hotel, dusk was just beginning to shade the eastern sky above the Sangre de Cristo Mountains. Leaving his saddle gear in the care of the stableman, but carrying his saddlebags and rifle, Longarm walked across the narrow alley that separated the sprawling adobe hotel from the stables and went through the spacious tile-paved lobby to the registration desk.

"I guess you got a room I can rent for a night or two?" he asked the clerk.

"Why, certainly, sir. If you'll just sign the register..." The clerk turned the big guest ledger around, dipped a pen in the inkwell that stood beside the register, and handed the pen to Longarm. "Sign on the first vacant line, if you please."

Longarm took the pen and glanced down at the register, his hand poised and ready to write. Just as he lowered the pen-point to the page, the signature on the line above the one he was about to fill caught his eye. His hand stopped in mid-air as he stared at the name written there.

"Do you mind telling me exactly what's going on here?" he asked the clerk, masking his surprise.

"I'm sorry, sir. I don't understand," the man frowned.

Longarm pointed to the signature that had caught his eye. "I mean that name right here on this bottom line."

Turning the register around again, the desk clerk looked at the page and said, "I don't see anything unusual, sir. It's just another guest signature. Deputy U. S. Marshal Custis Long signed in and was given room 208."

"That's what I'm talking about," Longarm nodded. "What did this fellow Long look like?"

"Why—I'm sorry, but I can't tell you that," the clerk replied. "I just came on duty about ten minutes ago, and I didn't see him. The clerk who had charge of the desk before I came on registered Marshal Long."

"That'd've been before the stage pulled in from Lamy?"

"Oh, yes, sir. The stage has just arrived."

"I know. I rode in on it." Longarm felt that he needed a moment to think. He took out a cigar and lighted it, ignoring the desk clerk's puzzled frown. Then he said, "I better have a little talk with that clerk who was on duty ahead of you. Just ask him to step out here a minute, if you don't mind."

"I—I'm sorry, sir, but he's already left the hotel. Is there something I can do?"

"Maybe you can find somebody else who'd be able to tell me what this fellow that signed the register looks like?"

"Why, I don't think that would be possible, sir. There'd have been a bellboy who took the guest's baggage upstairs, but he went off duty when the shifts changed, just as the desk clerk did." When Longarm did not reply, the clerk went on, "I'm afraid I still don't understand your concern, sir. Perhaps if you'd tell me why that signature seems to bother you—"

"I guess maybe I better." Longarm took his flat leather wallet from his inside coat pocket and flipped it open to show his badge. "I'm wondering just who in hell signed that register because I happen to be Deputy U. S. Marshal Custis Long, and I want to find out who's using my name."

"Oh, my God!" the desk clerk gasped, staring at the badge inscribed with Longarm's name. "You think the guest in Room 208 is an imposter?"

"I'd say it's a dead-on cinch he is," Longarm replied. "I might not be the only man in the country named Custis Long, but I damned sure know I'm the only U. S. marshal by that name."

"Yes, of course," the clerk agreed quickly. He looked at the signature, then back at Longarm, and asked, "What do you think we should do, Marshal Long?"

"I guess you've got a house detective here?" Longarm asked.

"I'm afraid we haven't. La Fonda's never found it necessary to have one. You understand, Marshal Long, we're not like the average hotel in a big city. Our guests are people on a vacation, sightseeing, things of that kind. We seldom get the riffraff that metropolitan hotels attract. But if you want somebody to help you—"

"I wasn't hinting for help," Longarm broke in. "I wanted to find out so I could tell him to keep out of my way."

"You mean that you're going up yourself to find out?"

"Maybe you've got a better idea? If whoever's in that room was just impersonating a U. S. marshal, I'd have to investigate him, even if he wasn't using my name in whatever scheme he's hatching up."

"Of course," the desk clerk nodded. "I understand that."

"Now, I better find out something first," Longarm went on. "How about the rooms on the sides of 208? And the ones across the hall? Anybody in them?"

"Just a moment," the clerk replied. He stepped to one side of the desk and consulted a chart on the wall, then turned back to Longarm. "Room 208 is at the end of the hall, Marshal Long. It's the only one on that corridor that's occupied. The rooms on both sides and across the hall are vacant."

"Good," Longarm said. "You just keep anybody from following me upstairs, then."

"Is there anything else I can do to help, Marshal?"

"If you're asking do I want you to go along, I don't. You stay right where you are, and keep anybody from following me up them stairs. I'll leave my rifle and saddlebags with you. Oh, yes. There's one thing I might find handy. I guess you got a spare key to Room 208? Or a pass key that'll open the door?"

"We have both spare keys and master keys, Marshal. Which would you prefer?"

"Whichever you got handy. Just give me the key, and stay out of my way while I go see what I can find out."

Longarm took the key which the clerk produced from a drawer and started across the lobby to the stairway. Having stayed at La Fonda during previous visits to Santa Fe, he was reasonably familiar with the hotel's layout. He walked down the corridor to Room 208, his footsteps whisper-quiet on the carpeted floor. A few paces from the door bearing the number 208, he stopped and slid out of his long black coat, letting it fall to a heap on the floor when he resumed his silent advance.

At the door of the room he stopped and pressed his ear to the wooden panel. If the room was occupied, there was no sound of any movement from its occupant. He inserted the pass key into the lock, but when he slid it forward only its tip entered the keyhole before he heard the tiny metallic click that told him it had encountered a key inserted from inside the door.

After he'd removed the useless key and pocketed it, Longarm stood frowning at the wooden portal for several moments. There was no way he could see to make a silent entry. He pressed his ear to the door again, but still heard no sound.

There's got to be somebody in that room, old son, he told himself silently. *Otherwise there wouldn't be no key in the lock. And seeing as that's the case, you're just going to have to take your chances.*

Drawing his Colt as he moved, Longarm stepped to one side of the door to be out of the line of fire if whoever was inside loosed a shot through the panels. Then he knocked gently.

There was no reply. Longarm risked leaning forward and pressed his ear to the panels again. He could not be sure, but thought he heard a faint sound of someone moving inside the room. Stepping aside, he knocked again, this time an author-itatively official rapping.

When his second series of knocks brought no response, Longarm called, "You in the room! This is Deputy United States Marshal Custis Long! Open the door and come out with your hands up!"

There was no reply from the room, but now Longarm was sure he could hear muffled sounds of movement inside. He levelled his Colt at the door and waited. A key grated in the lock, and Longarm's forefinger tensed on the Colt's trigger. The door swung halfway open, but whoever had opened it was standing behind it. He tried to peer around its edge, but he could not stretch his neck far enough to look inside.

"I got a gun covering you," Longarm said quietly. "If you got a gun, throw it out in the hall, and then step out here with your hands up!"

Beyond the door, a woman's voice said quietly, "I don't have a gun, Longarm, and you won't need one. I'll be very glad to surrender to you."

Longarm's jaw dropped and he let his Colt sag in his hand. Though a long while had passed since he'd heard the voice, he recognized it at once.

"Teena?" he called. "Cristina Albee?"

"I don't know who else you'd be expecting to greet you like this in Santa Fe," the woman replied. "If I thought you were expecting somebody else to be waiting for you, I think I might be jealous. But do come in, Longarm. I've been waiting for you for almost two hours.

Chapter 4

Stopping only long enough to scoop his coat up from the floor, Longarm went into Room 208. Cristina Albee was standing just past the edge of the open door, and she had changed not at all from the way Longarm remembered her. The long blonde hair that hung down to her shoulders framed her oval face, with its luminous brown eyes, thin uptilted nose, and lusciously full, pouting lips. She was wearing a diaphanous silk dressing gown, and through its translucent fabric Longarm could see the budded pink tips of her small high-standing breasts, her narrow tapered waist and flaring hips.

With a single swift move, Cristina pushed the door closed and extended her arms. Letting his coat fall to the floor, Longarm swept her to him and bent to kiss her. They held the kiss, their questing tongues entwining, until both were breathless. Longarm released her reluctantly, and took a backward step to look at her.

"I don't mind telling you, you're a real sight for sore eyes, Teena," he said. "I thought about you a lot on the train on the way from Denver, but I sure didn't expect you to be waiting for me. How'd you know I was coming to Santa Fe? And when I'd get in?"

"Having the governor of the Territory for an uncle makes a lot of things possible," Teena replied. "Your chief in Denver sent a wire to the chief marshal here, saying you were on the way, and Uncle Lew got word about the message." Then, with a little frown, she asked, "Now you tell me something, Longarm. Would you really have shot through the door if I hadn't opened it when I did?"

"If you'd kept me waiting another minute, I'd've put a bullet through it, and don't you ever doubt it."

"I was pretty sure you would. But why shoot somebody you couldn't see?"

"You oughta know the answer to that, Teena. There's lots of people carrying grudges against me, just like they do against any lawman. For all I knew, there might've been one of them behind that door."

"My idea was to give you a little surprise," she smiled. "I think I did, too."

"But if you'd been somebody else, it'd have been a different kind of surprise," he reminded her.

"Of course. When I planned my surprise greeting, it didn't occur to me how you'd react to it."

"I'd a lot sooner have your kind of welcome than the kind I figured I was about to get," Longarm told her. "But what're you doing back in Santa Fe, Teena? You was planning to go live in Europe the last I knew."

"I did," she nodded. "In fact, I just got back to Santa Fe a couple of weeks ago. But . . . Well, it's a long story, and I'm sure you'd like a drink after that dusty ride on the stage from Lamy. Come on. I've got a bottle of your favorite Maryland rye whiskey and a bottle of champagne for myself."

Taking Longarm's hand, she led him to a velvet-upholstered sofa that stood in front of the domed adobe fireplace in the inside corner of the room. An ice bucket held a bottle of champagne, and beside it stood a bottle of Tom Moore and glasses. Longarm opened the wine and filled a glass for Teena before pulling the cork from the whiskey bottle and pouring himself a drink.

"You know, I got more than just a hunch that you had something to do with me being put on this case," he told Teena as he took off his vest, unbuckled his gunbelt, and hung them on a chair before sitting down beside her. "Your uncle holding the job he does and all like that."

"It was Uncle Lew's idea, really," Teena replied. "He and Terry Higgins decided you were the man they needed on this case even before I heard anything about it. Of course, I didn't discourage them when Uncle Lew told me they were going to ask the attorney general to send you here to work on it."

It had been several years earlier when Longarm had first

met Teena and her uncle, General Lew Wallace, the governor of New Mexico Territory. Longarm's assignment then had been to help the territorial authorities break up the vicious and corrupt Santa Fe Ring, a group of powerful politicians and landowners. Through its covert control of the Territorial Legislature and key county offices, the Ring fattened on graft that its members extracted from virtually everyone wishing to do business in the territory.

In the course of carrying out his assignment, Longarm had also met Sergeant Terence Higgins, the governor's aide. He and Higgins had not only worked together in smashing the Ring's power, but had rescued Teena after she'd been captured by a rebellious outlaw band of Jicarilla Apaches. The Indians had taken her to a remote hideaway in the northern Sangre de Cristo Mountains, and after an anxious day and night of sniping Longarm and Higgins had managed to free her from the Indians and bring her back safely to Santa Fe.

"Well, you could've brushed me off my feet with a feather when I seen you," Longarm told Teena now. "I just figured you'd still be in Europe, drawing and painting and all like that."

"I think I'm about ready to give up any hope of becoming a first-rate artist," Teena said. "After seeing some of the work the best painters and sculptors are producing today, I just don't believe I could ever measure up."

"I thought the picture you drawed of me when we stopped in Trinidad that time was real good," Longarm assured her.

Teena smiled across the rim of her glass. "I still have it tucked away in my portfolio, Longarm. But you never did keep your promise to pose for me nude. I've had to rely on my memory to remember you the way I like you best." She put her glass on the table and leaned toward him. "We can talk later. Right now I want to find out if what I remember is right."

Longarm needed no further invitation. He pulled Teena to him and sought her lips. Her tongue darted into his mouth and as they held the kiss her hands moved busily over his chest, opening his buttons to reach and touch Longarm's skin. After a few moments of rubbing her soft fingers through the wiry brush on his chest, she broke their kiss and moved her attentions

33

to his trousers. Unbuckling his belt, she opened his fly to free the jutting shaft that had swelled and grown erect as their kisses were prolonged.

While Teena's soft hands roamed from Longarm's chest to his crotch, he was refreshing his memories of her small, perfect body with his lips and fingertips. Pushing aside the thin, filmy silk negligee, he brushed his lips along her smooth white neck and shoulders before trailing his caresses down to the protruding pink tips of her firm, upstanding breasts.

Teena shivered as Longarm's tongue found the tips that had emerged from the pebbled rosettes crowning her small, rounded globes. Her hands closed tightly around his shaft and her body writhed as he prolonged his attentions.

"Take me to bed, Longarm!" she gasped. "I've been sitting here waiting for you almost two hours, and all the time I've been remembering our afternoon in the mountains above Trinidad and the night we spent later, here in this very room. If I don't feel you inside of me real soon, I'm going to explode!"

Longarm levered out of his boots. When he stood up his clothing, already loosened by Teena, fell away to the floor. As he picked her up, the filmy negligee slid from her shoulders and fell to the floor as he lowered her to the waiting bed.

Teena stretched her arms up and pulled him down to her. He felt her soft fingers grasping his jutting erection and then the moist warmth that had been waiting behind her golden fleece engulfed his rigid shaft as he lunged.

"Oh, yes!" Teena gasped as she brought her hips up to meet his drive. "This is even better than I remembered, Longarm! I'm going to explode anyhow, in just a minute, but don't stop! I want to be here with you in me for a long, long time!"

"Don't worry, Teena," he assured her. He began a long, slow stroking that brought small cries of joy bubbling from her throat. "I ain't in a hurry."

"No, but I am!" she breathed as she writhed ecstatically while he continued his full, deep thrusts. "I am right—now, now, Longarm!"

A whimpering scream cut off Teena's words and for a few moments Longarm speeded up his strokes to match her frantic writhing. Her cries of ecstasy faded into soft, contented moans, and Longarm stopped driving. He held himself pressed firmly against her until the last small shudders of her frantic spasm faded and she lay quietly, her eyes closed, her lips parted in a smile of satisfaction. After a while she opened her eyes and looked up at him.

"Oh, that was lovely, Longarm!" she sighed. "But it was over too quick. And I know you're not satisfied, because I can feel you're still hard."

"Don't let that fret you a bit, Teena. I ain't going to quit on you."

"I know. I remember every minute we spent together, in the mountains at Trinidad, and here in the hotel later on."

"Well, I ain't exactly forgot you, either."

"Then you'll remember what I enjoyed so much."

"Seems to me we both enjoyed every bit of the time we had together, Teena.

"We did. But on the mountainside at Trinidad, where we didn't have a bed or even a blanket to spread on that rough rocky ground—remember, Longarm?—you picked me up and held me and I felt like I was floating all the time. . . ." Teena's words trailed off into silence. She looked questioningly up at Longarm, her eyes shining and her full lips glistening.

"Is that what you'd like to do now?" Longarm asked.

"You don't mind, do you?"

"Of course I don't. Whatever pleasures you, pleasures me."

Longarm clasped Teena closely to his chest and held her while he lifted himself off the bed, carrying her with him. She put her hands on his shoulders and levered herself up, straddling his hips. Reaching around her, Longarm clasped her firmly rounded buttocks in his strong hands and held her suspended while Teena gazed at him with a smile of anticipation.

She freed one of her clasped hands and reached between their bodies to position Longarm's engorged shaft, then began tightening her legs to pull herself closer to him. Longarm spread his feet as the balance of their bodies changed, and braced himself as Teena leaned back, her hands locked around his neck, her body glued to his.

35

"Ah," she sighed. "This is glorious, Longarm—nothing to take my mind away from the feeling of you filling me completely!"

Longarm bent forward to kiss her. As their lips met and their darting tongues entwined, Teena began rocking her hips. She moved slowly at first, pressing her pubis firmly against his groin, but soon she speeded up and in a few more moments her movements became faster and still faster until her small body was writhing in a frenzy of passion.

Her rhythmic rocking gave way to spasmodic jerks until she cried out and shuddered, her head thrown back, her body quivering. Still impaled on Longarm's rigid shaft, she leaned forward until her head rested on Longarm's shoulder and her full breasts were pressed to his muscular chest.

She held herself pressed against him until her frantic spasms subsided and her body stopped trembling, then raised her head and whispered in his ear, "You still didn't let go, Longarm. I hope that means you want me to keep on."

"If you feel like it," he said. "I'm enjoying this as much as you are."

"Once more, then," Teena said. "Then we can go back to the bed and rest a while."

From the avidity with which Teena began gyrating her hips again, Longarm judged that she needed no rest as yet. He let her set the rhythm of their movements, holding her quivering buttocks firmly while Teena swung her body back and forth on his impaling shaft.

She maintained her writhings longer this time, and Longarm held himself in firm control until small screams started pouring from Teena's lips again and her frenzied, twisting hips were rolling in spasmodic jerks from side to side while she pressed down on his still-rigid sex. Her cries had risen to a crescendo, and her small body was quivering in frantic, triphammer-fast jerkings when he let go his control. Then, as he jetted, Longarm pulled Teena to him and held her pressed firmly to his chest until his own spasm passed, and hers ebbed into an occasional involuntary twitching.

When Teena's breathing grew more regular and her body had frozen into the immobility of an ivory statue, Longarm stepped back to the bed and bent forward, lowering them both to the mattress without breaking their fleshly joining. Teena's eyes were closed, her lips parted, her breathing gusty.

Longarm rested only part of his weight on her, supporting himself on his elbows, Teena's head nestled in the pulsing hollow between his neck and shoulder. She did not move for a long time, but at last she sighed and moved her head so that she could look up into his eyes.

"What a lovely man you are, Longarm," she whispered. "You're still not ready to quit, are you?"

"I can start again if you want me to."

"Yes. Whenever you feel like it. You've already pleased me more than any man I've ever known, but I guess I'm just greedy."

She grasped his cheeks between her hands and pulled his head down until their lips met. While their questing tongues entwined and probed, Longarm kept up the rhythmic stroking he'd begun, and this time he relaxed his control as Teena's head arched back and broke their kiss.

Longarm drove steadily, with deep full thrusts, speeding his tempo as Teena's response began. When once more she mounted to the brink of satisfaction and with her final joyful scream broke the room's quiet air, he waited until her orgasm had reached its peak before jetting into his own final spasm of satisfied completion.

They lay quietly for a while, in the relaxed contentment of lovers who have been reunited after a long absence. Then Teena stirred and said, "I think I'd like another glass of champagne, Longarm, before we get started again. Besides, I know you want to talk about this case that's brought you back here."

"Why, there ain't no hurry about that," he told her. "I figure your uncle can tell me about it when I see him."

"That's one of the reasons we need to talk now," she said, getting off the bed and moving to the divan.

She glanced at her negligee where it lay crumpled on the floor but made no move to pick it up. Longarm started toward the divan, stopped by the heap of clothing he'd discarded in such a hurry, and reached down to pick up his longjohns.

"Don't bother," Teena said. "You know a naked man isn't

anything new to me. Besides, with all those beautiful muscles you've got, you look so much better than most of the models and other men I've seen without their clothes on that I enjoy just looking at you."

"If it pleasures you to look, I sure don't want to spoil anything you enjoy," Longarm told her. He stopped at the chair where he'd hung his vest long enough to take out a cigar and light it, then sat down beside Teena on the divan. She'd filled her champagne glass and Longarm's shot glass. He took a sip of the mellow but sharp Maryland rye, then set the glass down and turned to Teena.

"Whatever it is you want to talk about must be right important," he suggested.

"It is," she replied. "And I don't want to have to talk about it later. All I really want to do is enjoy being with you in bed. But a lot of things have changed since you were here before, Longarm."

"Such as what?"

"Well, the biggest change is that Uncle Lew has resigned as territorial governor."

"I'm right sorry to hear that," Longarm frowned. "He's about the smartest man I ever run into, and I was sorta figuring on having him fill me in on this railroad case. But I reckon Sergeant Higgins will stay on, and he'll know all about it, being your uncle's aide. How's the sergeant doing, Teena? Did he get that promotion to master sergeant he was bucking for?"

"You haven't heard about Terry, either?"

Longarm shook his head, then said, "You don't mean to tell me he'll be going back East with your uncle?"

"Of course not. You see, Terry's not just Sergeant Higgins any more. When old Marshal Otero died, Uncle Lew had the President appoint Terry to be chief U. S. marshal for the territory."

Longarm's jaw dropped in surprise, but he recovered quickly and said, "He'll be my boss on this case, then. And I can't say I'd ever hope for a better one."

Teena sighed with relief. "I've been halfway dreading to tell you that, Longarm. I was afraid you might be jealous about Terry's promotion."

"Now, why in tunket would you think that?"

"Well, you've had so much more experience—"

"Hold on right there, Teena," Longarm broke in. "I guess I better explain something to you."

"Go ahead."

"I wouldn't take a chief marshal's job if the President himself got on his knees and begged me to. That ain't the sorta work I'm cut out for."

"But you're so good at what you do!" she protested.

"Maybe so. But I can't send a man out on a case where he might get shot up and killed unless I can go along and stand with him when the bullets is flying. And I ain't any good at all when it comes to juggling papers the way I watch my chief doing. I'd go crazy in less'n a week. I just wasn't put together that way, Teena, and I got sense enough to know it."

Teena was silent for a moment. Then she leaned over and kissed Longarm, a soft and gentle kiss without the urgency of passion that had marked her earlier caresses. "I know you're about the bravest man I've ever met, Longarm," she said softly. "And now I think you're a pretty wise one, too. It takes wisdom and courage both to tell me what you just said."

"Now, that's enough of that kinda talk, Teena," Longarm told her sternly. "Let's get back to this business about the railroads. That's what I'm here for."

"Well, all that I know about it is what Uncle Lew's told me, and that's little enough. I was worried about the way you'd feel when you found out that Terry was going to be . . . well, as the army says, higher than your rank in the chain of command."

"But you're not worrying about it any more?"

Teena shook her head. "Not after what you just told me. I ought to have known you'd accept the situation.

"I just asked you about the railroad case because I figured it was on your mind," Longarm said. "I figured that maybe you'd heard the general say something that might help me understand it better."

Teena shook her head. "We haven't even mentioned railroads since Uncle Lew first told me about the decision he and Terry had made in asking the attorney general to assign you to the case."

"Let's don't waste any more time talking about it, then. I

guess you got a pretty big job on your hands, helping General Wallace get ready to move, with his books and all like that to take care of."

"He's been packing his books and papers. I've been looking after the furniture and things of that sort," Teena explained. "We've barely had time to talk to each other."

"How much longer is he going to be here?"

"He wants to stay until the new governor arrives. That'll probably be in a week or so."

"And I guess you'll be going back East with him?"

"Farther than just back East, Longarm. You see, he's been appointed to the United States Ambassador to Turkey, and I'm going with him to be his official hostess at the embassy."

"All the way to Turkey? Why, that's halfway around the world!"

"Yes, I know. That's why I took this room in your name, because I wanted to spend some time with you before we both got too busy with our other affairs."

"You don't stay still a minute, do you, Teena?" Longarm asked. "Last time you up and took off for Europe; now you're going even farther away."

"I guess that's just how things happen," Teena replied. She leaned toward him, her lips and eyes inviting. "Let's forget everything else now and go back to bed, Longarm. We've got tonight ahead of us, and I'm not going to worry any more about all the tomorrows."

Chapter 5

Longarm came out of La Fonda and stopped at the corner of Santa Fe's central plaza to light an after-breakfast cigar. Teena had roused when the faint chiming of the bells in the tower of San Fernando Cathedral reached into the pre-dawn shadows of their room. She'd kissed Longarm good morning when she slipped out of bed, dressed hurriedly, and kissed him goodbye with a whispered promise that they would find a way to meet again later in the day. His cigar lighted, Longarm flicked away the match and started diagonally across the plaza.

Both the tree-dappled square and the streets that defined it were deserted in spite of the late hour, though the shops that bordered three of the plaza's sides were open for business. Strolling unhurriedly, Longarm made his way to the Palace of the Governors, which stretched along one entire side of the plaza. The sun hung high above the ancient adobe building's flat roof, throwing its facade into shadow, the shadow made deeper by the overhang of its second story, which transformed the street-level front into a sort of porch.

Reaching the ornately carved double doors of the palace, Longarm passed through them into the wide entry that led to the central hall which ran from end to end of the building. He strode along the corridor until he found the door he sought, the door that bore the inscription "Chief United States Marshal— Territory of New Mexico." He knocked twice, a token tapping of his knuckles, before opening the door and entering.

Terence Higgins was rising to his feet behind the flat-topped desk that dominated the room. The desk reminded Longarm of the one in Billy Vail's office in Denver; it was piled high with papers that covered its top.

"Don't bother coming to the door," Longarm told Higgins.

"Longarm!" Higgins exclaimed. There was a touch of Irish

brogue a generation removed from the auld sod in his voice. He leaned across the desk, his hand extended, as he went on, "I was wondering if it wasn't about time for you to get here."

"This ain't the easiest town in the country to get to on a train, you know," Longarm said, shaking Higgins's hand. "I'd rather ride a burro up Cheyenne Mountain than that rattletrap stage down here from Lamy."

Longarm was studying Higgins's face as he spoke. He found it little changed from their previous meeting. There were a few wrinkles around the young man's eyes that hadn't been there before, and a new firmness to his square jutting chin, but his red hair was as crinkled-curly as ever, and his wide welcoming grin as friendly.

"Sit down, Longarm," Higgins said, waving to a chair at the corner of the desk. "I was beginning to think that you might be away from Denver on a case. It's been almost two weeks since the governor wired Washington asking them to send you here."

"Anything that goes through Washington takes at least that long to get anybody's attention," Longarm smiled. "Governor Wallace must've done some pretty strong persuading to get me here this fast."

"Well, you're not a minute too early," Higgins said. He started to add something more, thought better of it, and a frown drew his bushy red eyebrows together. After a minute he went on, "I hope you didn't mind me asking for you, Longarm. I know you've been with the marshal's force a lot longer than I have, and I was afraid that maybe . . ." He hesitated, shook his head, and went on, "Just forget what I was about to say. I'm damned glad to see you."

"Maybe I oughta finish what you started to tell me," Longarm suggested. "What you're getting at is that on account of I been a deputy marshal for quite a spell, I might figure I was due for a job like you got now. Well, rest easy, Terry. I don't want to be anything but what I am right now. Even if I was to be offered the job you got, I wouldn't take it. I ain't cut out to set behind a desk and fight papers. Does that make you feel any better?"

"It does, and I'm damned glad you came out with it. But when you were here before, I was just a paper-pushing sergeant in the army, and I was afraid you might—"

"Be a little jealous?" Longarm finished for him. He shook his head. "Not for a minute. Now, we got that outa the way, so let's get down to business. From what Billy Vail told me, you're in a hurry to get this case I'm here on closed up fast. Am I right?"

"You certainly are," Higgins nodded. "I don't know whether Marshal Vail mentioned it, but the deal between the Santa Fe and the Southern Pacific has to be closed before the end of this month, and they're both pushing me pretty hard."

"And both of 'em swings a pretty big stick back in Washington, too," Longarm added. "I got more'n a hunch that's why the men back there got busy faster than they generally do."

"I'm sure you're right," Higgins agreed. He picked up a stack of papers from the desk and asked, "How much do you know about the case?"

"Not as much as I'll need to. Billy Vail told me a little bit, but that was mostly about the fight that's been going on between the Sante Fe and the Southern Pacific. He didn't have much to say outside of that."

"You do know that there's two million dollars' worth of Atlantic & Pacific Railroad bonds and another two million in U. S. Treasury bonds missing, don't you?"

"Oh, sure. And Billy told me about that copy of the treaty with Mexico that was along with the bonds. But that don't help me much, Terry. I wanta know who was supposed to be in charge of them bonds and where they come from and how they was sent and when they was missed. For all I know now, that stuff might just have been mislaid, not stolen."

"I don't think that's the case," Higgins said. "The bonds and the copy of the treaty with Mexico were in a suitcase that had specially fitted locks. The suitcase was packed and locked in the Santa Fe's main office in Chicago."

"Who handled the suitcase last? Some ten-dollar-a-week clerk, or a high muckety-muck from the railroad?"

"I suppose there were some clerks around when the suitcase was closed and locked, but the Santa Fe's treasurer was the man who packed them, and he was the one who locked the suitcase."

"Well, if they could trust anybody, I expect it'd be him," Longarm frowned. "But that's one hell of a lot of money. It'd be a real temptation for just about anybody."

"It might be if it'd been cash instead of bonds," Higgins agreed. "But those A&P bonds aren't worth a dime to anybody except the Santa Fe or the SP, and I'd like to see somebody take a two-million-dollar U. S. Treasury bond into a bank and try to get it cashed without a lot of questions being asked."

"You're right about that, Terry," Longarm nodded. "But I wasn't thinking about anybody trying to *sell* them Treasury bonds. A smart man that knows his way around would be more likely to use them bonds for security to get a whopping big loan."

"Which would be as good as cash, I suppose," Higgins nodded. "But the serial numbers of the bonds are being sent out to every bank in the country. They'd be spotted in a minute."

"There's forgers who can change them serial numbers," Longarm reminded Higgins. "And something else came into my mind while I was on my way down here from Denver. The Santa Fe's caught between a rock and a hard place as long as them bonds is missing. How much do you figure they'd pay to get 'em back?"

"Quite a lot, I'd say. But so far nobody's asked about a reward for returning them."

"Well, it ain't too late for that to happen yet. As far as that treaty, I figure it was just stolen because it was in the same suitcase with the bonds, but if whoever stole the stuff finds out what the treaty's good for, that'd be something they could use to boost up a ransom."

"It's a good theory, I'll grant you," Higgins agreed. "Except that nobody's made any demands."

Longarm replied with a nod. He was touching a match to a fresh cigar. Then, through a cloud of blue smoke, he asked, "Who was supposed to bring them bonds here from Chicago,

Terry? I don't expect they just shipped that suitcase along with ordinary baggage?"

"Of course not. The Santa Fe hired Allan Pinkerton's detective agency to handle the delivery."

"I'd say we don't need to waste any time tracing the suitcase every inch of the way from Chicago, then," Longarm said. "Pinkerton's got about the best reputation of anybody in that line of work."

"There's always a first time for anybody to slip up," Higgins reminded Longarm.

"Oh, sure. I won't mark 'em off of my list till I'm sure some bad apple didn't get into Pinkerton's barrel," Longarm assured Higgins. "Now, maybe you better tell me what happened after the suitcase got out here from Chicago."

"That won't take long," Higgins replied. "Pinkerton's man kept the suitcase with him every mile of the way. He didn't have a key to it. He handed it over to the station agent at Deming and got a receipt, and he swears that from the time he left Chicago until he delivered it the bag wasn't out of his sight for a minute. After he delivered it at Deming—"

"Wait a minute," Longarm broke in. "Deming's the name of a town, I guess, but I never heard of it before."

"It's a town, but it's new. And it's no wonder that you haven't heard of it, because it's not on the maps yet. You've seen places like it before, I'm sure—towns that grew up at a railhead."

"How far west from Albuquerque is it?"

"A hell of a long way," Higgins answered. "You're thinking Deming's on the Santa Fe main line, but it's not. It's on the southern spur they started building southwest from Albuquerque to connect with the Atlantic & Pacific tracks into Mexico."

"I didn't even know the Santa Fe had any tracks in the territory except for their main line," Longarm frowned.

"They started it right after they bought the A&P, to give them a connection into Mexico," Higgins explained. "Then, from what I've heard, they ran so short of money that they had to stop construction. Deming grew up around the old railhead."

"That means I got to spend some extra time learning the lay

of the land down there, then," Longarm said thoughtfully. "I just taken for granted it was in country I'd learned when I was on that case you know about, down west of Albuquerque."

"It's further south, Longarm. The spur follows the Rio Grande south from Albuquerque for about a hundred miles, then runs fifty or so miles to the east. That's where Deming is."

"That's pretty far south," Longarm frowned. "It seems to me the Santa Fe'd have the government on their necks for being too close to the SP."

"They got around that two-hundred-mile north-south separation law by calling the new tracks a spur to connect with the A&P into Mexico," Higgins explained. "Don't ask me what strings they pulled to get it approved."

"I don't need to, Terry. I got a pretty good idea. When Billy Vail said this case was at the Santa Fe's railhead, I just got the idea it was on the main line. Not that it makes much nevermind."

"I suppose not," Higgins nodded.

"You'll have a deputy someplace close around Deming, I guess?" Longarm asked.

Higgins shook his head. "No. My closest deputy's in Las Cruces, down by El Paso. I'm afraid you can't count on him for anything; right now he's on a smuggling case over in the Pecos River country. Not that I think you'd need any help, from what I saw of the way you handled those Jicarilla Apaches the last time you were here."

"You had a lot to do with that one turning out so good," Longarm said. "And neither one of us might've come out with whole skins if it hadn't been for old Esquivel being mad as he was at the Apaches."

"I think we both feel that way," Higgins nodded.

Longarm broke the silence that followed as both men recalled the case they'd worked on together. He asked, "I don't guess there's much more you can tell me, is there?"

"I'm afraid not."

"I'll be on my way, then." Longarm stood up. "I'd imagine the Santa Fe's got a telegraph wire to Deming?"

"Oh, of course," Higgins nodded. "But any wire you'd send me would have to be delivered by the stage from Lamy. To save you asking, if I get any more information that might help you, I'll sure send you a wire."

"You do that." Longarm extended his hand and Higgins shook it. Then he went on, "If anything else comes to mind, I'll be in town till the stage leaves for Lamy. You'll find me at La Fonda or at Governor Wallace's house. I got to stop by there and say goodbye to Teena."

"I'll find you if I need you," Higgins said. "And good luck, Longarm."

"Thanks. The way this case is shaping up, I got an idea I'll need more luck than anything else to close it. But luck or not, Terry, you can bet your bottom dollar it'll be closed!"

Travelling on a train that operated without a schedule and was destined to stop in the middle of nowhere wasn't a new experience for Longarm. Just the same, he chafed as the four-car accommodation train chugged with slow deliberation for almost a full day along the western bank of the Rio Grande over tracks that hadn't been fully ballasted. The rails had seen so little use that they were still crusted with foundry-scale, and the rickety cars thunked almost constantly as they swayed on a winding course dictated by the sinuous riverbed until the tracks curved west into the sinking sun.

There was nothing but monotony in the changing vista he saw through the dirt-streaked windows of the ancient day coach. As long as the tracks ran close to the river, there had been signs of civilization. The train had stopped briefly at half a dozen tiny towns to discharge freight and let passengers alight. Between the towns there had been a few small adobe houses spaced at long intervals beside the stream, the houses set in a pattern formed by the crisscrossing *acequias* that carried water from the river to the patchwork of faded green fields that surrounded each house.

After the railroad tracks left the river, there were no more towns or houses. There were signs that civilization had advanced with the tracks, the debris left from construction at each place where a railhead camp had been established. For the most part, though, all the landscape afforded was a vista of undulating ocher earth cut by an occasional streak of soil that varied from a brownish-gray to purplish-red before petering out and merging into the predominantly yellowish landscape.

When the accommodation train came to a final halt at Deming, the sun was hanging only a hand's-breadth above the flat line of the horizon. Longarm gathered up his gear, saddle and saddlebags, rifle and bedroll, and swung out of the ramshackle coach. The depot was small and the platform even smaller, but that did not matter, since he was the only passenger to alight. He stood at the edge of the platform and looked around the town.

For convenience, Longarm divided the towns where he'd been sent on cases into two categories. One was the both-sides-of-the-track, which applied to older communities built up almost equally on either side of the railroad depot. The second was one-side-of-the-track towns, in which building had been confined to a single side of the rails, and Deming fell into this latter category.

Stretching away from the tracks were the saloons and stores that made up the new town. Those nearest the tracks were generally shabbier, and he could identify some as being left-overs from Deming's Hell-on-Wheels era, shanties which had inched along from week to week or month to month paralleling the rails as they advanced.

Hell on Wheels was the term which had become attached to the railhead towns which had sprung up everywhere in the West as the railroads pushed their tracks across the prairies and over the mountains toward the Pacific. They were mobile communities, populated largely by riffraff: gamblers, sharpsters, and whores who preyed on the construction crews; saloon-keepers and quick-dealing itinerant merchants who sold shoddy goods at inflated prices to the crews who had no other place to buy their needs.

Built or adapted to move with the advancing railhead, most of the buildings belonging to the Hell-on-Wheels era were small huts mounted on expanded wagonbeds. Some, however, were simply board storefronts or saloon-fronts erected as the entrances to big tents, and many Hell-on-Wheels residents made no effort to put up a front, but simply lived and worked in tents.

Virtually all the structures Longarm saw were small and new. The exceptions were the two largest buildings. They were about the same size—each had two stories—but one was shabby while the other shone with fresh paint, white with black trim, which glistened in the low-hanging sun. The remaining buildings were houses, and these were generally small. Only a handful of them were new; for the most part, these were the ones which stood farthest from the tracks. A few glowed with the golden tan of freshly milled and as yet unpainted boards, while the remainder shone with fresh paint, as did the big new structure close to the railroad depot.

When he'd completed his examination of the town itself, Longarm turned to look on the opposite side of the tracks. Here he saw the orderly disorder that marked all railhead construction camps: an area filled with head-high stacks of crossties, beyond it another devoted to rectangles of stockpiled rails, and closest to the tracks the big shanty-like warehouses and tool sheds and smaller structures that housed the shops and foundry.

Spur tracks and sidings ran from the main line to the yards, and on one of the spurs nearest the depot there were half a dozen spurs on which stood boxcars that had been converted to sleeping quarters and offices for the railroad employees who remained after construction had been halted. Longarm studied these for a moment, then picked up his gear and went into the depot.

Small as the building was, it had been partitioned into two rooms. The one in which Longarm stood served as an office and waiting room and held the telegraph key behind a counter; the other, its interior visible through a connecting door, did duty as a baggage room. A man wearing the woven wicker-topped cap issued to Santa Fe employees stood behind the counter thumbing through sheets of flimsy held on a clipboard.

"You the station agent?" Longarm asked.

"That's right. What d'you need, mister?"

"I guess there was some kind of boss that taken charge of the yards here when the construction stopped, wasn't there?"

"Yep. But if you're looking for work, it won't do you no good to bother him. We got all the guards and maintenance men we can use."

"A job ain't what I'm looking for. My name's Long. I'm a deputy United States marshal, and I was sent down here to find some Sante Fe property that was lost or got stolen."

"Oh, my God, yes!" the agent gasped. "The super's been keeping the wires hot, trying to get a line on when they'd send the man they promised us down here, and I guess you're him."

"I guess I am," Longarm nodded. "Now, what's your super's name, and where'll I find him?"

"His name's Frank Carstow, and you'll find him in that third passenger coach on the first siding past the depot."

Retracing his steps along the truncated depot platform, Longarm walked along the uneven roadbed to the car the station agent had indicated. Swinging up on the steps, he rapped at the door. There was no reply, and he pressed his face to the glass pane set in the door for a closer look. He saw a desk or table and a chair in the foreground, and realized then that the car was a gutted passenger coach remodeled with partitions into a mobile office and living quarters, the kind of car that moved with a construction camp to accommodate the job's superintendent.

When his second rat-a-tat of knocking brought no response, and he saw no sign of motion inside, Longarm decided to go into town, find a room, and come back later. He was turning away when his eyes caught a glimpse of something odd-looking on the floor. He moved closer, cocking his head to kill the reflection of his own face in the glass and to bring the object into better focus.

He could see then that what had caught his attention was a man's hand stretching from beneath the desk. The upturned hand was motionless, and by straining his eyes he could see that the sleeve on the few visible inches of the arm was stained with blood.

Old son, Longarm told himself, *it looks like you got here just a mite too late.*

Chapter 6

For the first time, Longarm tried the door leading into the office car. It turned readily. He went inside. The recumbent figure on the floor was fully visible now. Beyond the corpse, Longarm could see that what he'd taken for a desk was just a narrow table hinged to the wall, and that an overturned chair lay under it. The window above the table was broken and shards of glass lay on the tabletop, mingled with sheets of paper.

He hunkered down beside the corpse for a closer look. The dead man was coatless, the cuffs of his shirtsleeves turned up and the shoulders of the shirt blood-spattered, indicating that when the bullet which killed him struck he'd been sitting at the table, working. Glancing at the body, Longarm noted that the pool of blood that had gathered around the corpse's head was just starting to congeal. The dead man had been in his middle forties, Longarm judged. His face was clean-shaven, its features distorted by the death-dealing bullet that had passed through his head from the point of his jaw to the crown, where thin brown hair was matted around a shattered exit wound.

Easy enough to see what happened, Longarm told himself silently. *Poor fellow was just setting here working when some backshooting son of a bitch that'd been hiding out in that mess of railroad gear potted him through the window. Now, whoever shot him had to have a reason, so the first thing you got to do, old son, is to find out who this dead man was and why somebody'd wanta cut him down.*

Rising to his feet, Longarm surveyed the cubicle which had been created by partitioning the railroad coach. A cabinet, its door ajar, had been fitted into the partitioning wall. Glancing into the cubby, he saw shelves laden with stacks of letters, ledger sheets, and other paperwork, indicating that the room had been used as an office. A door was set into the partition at one side, near the opposite wall of the coach. Longarm stepped over to try the door and a fresh scar high in the wall caught his eye. He looked more closely and saw that it was a bullet hole.

Taking out his pocketknife, Longarm cut through the thin paneling and uncovered the slug lodged in the car's outer wall. He dug it out and held it in front of the window to examine it more closely. It was easily recognizable; although flattened at the nose, enough of the rifling marks remained to tell him that it had been fired from a Winchester.

Which don't mean too much, he told himself silently. *Just about everybody and his brother's got a Winchester. And whoever it was done the shooting was out there on the ground.*

He dropped the slug in his pocket and pushed through the partition door. The cubicle he had entered contained two bunks, the bedding of one rumpled, that on the second untouched.

Must've had the whole car to himself, Longarm deduced as he moved through the cubicle to a door at its rear. *Likely he's the superintendent, that Frank Carstow you was looking for.*

At the back of the sleeping compartment, a second door opened into a shelf-lined storage room. It was in total disarray now; the papers which had been on the shelves were scattered in heaps on the floor. The crumpled piles of paper almost hid the two leather suitcases that lay on the floor, their sides slashed to open gaping holes which showed their empty interiors.

Well, now, Longarm told himself as he squatted beside the slashed luggage for a closer examination, *it appears like you ain't the only one looking for them missing bonds, old son. It's a shiny gold eagle to a plugged penny that whoever killed that fellow come in here trying to find something, and it'd have to be them bonds he was after. Too bad there ain't no way of telling in this mess whether he found 'em or not.*

Rising to his feet, Longarm continued his investigation of the coach. The area behind the storage closet held a small coal-fired range and counters that from their appearance had been used for food preparation. Cabinets attached to the walls contained cooking utensils and china. Dust lay thick on the stove and counters, and cinders grated under this boot soles with each step he took.

This kitchen ain't been used for a while, Longarm deduced as he completed his investigations. *But that dead fellow was sure as hell the big boss here, or he wouldn't've had this kind of layout. And it looks like there ain't much more to see here, so you better hyper over to the depot and see if you can get some answers.*

Back at the little depot, the stationmaster was still working with the papers on his clipboard. He looked up and asked, "I guess you found Mr. Carstow all right?"

"Oh, I found him. Only he wasn't all right. He was dead. Somebody put a rifle bullet through his head."

"You mean—"

"I mean just what I said," Longarm broke in. "Now I got some questions for you to answer." He took out his wallet and showed the railroader his badge.

"Ask away, Marshal," the stationmaster said. "Only I got to hurry up and find Mr. Forbes so I can tell him about—"

"Forbes is next in charge after Carstow?" Longarm asked. When the railroader nodded Longarm went on, "I'll need to talk to him myself. From what you just said, you must have a pretty good idea where he'd be this time of day."

"Right after the accommodation started back to Albuquerque, he went up to the Harvey House; said he was going to have supper early."

"That'd be the big new white building just up the tracks?"

"That's it."

"Then I'll go find him," Longarm said. "Save you having to close down and go look for him."

"Marshal, this depot might as well be closed as open, with one train a day, and that one an accommodation," the stationmaster said. "I just set around and do nothing until tomorrow. But if you're going looking for George Forbes anyhow, that's fine."

"You got a safe place where I can leave my rifle and saddle gear?" Longarm asked. "A checkroom or something?"

"I'll stow it under the counter. It'll be safe there. I'll have to stay here anyhow, till you come back with Mr. Forbes."

Handing his gear over the counter, Longarm started toward the cluster of buildings north of the tracks. The distance was not great, and as soon as he'd stepped off the depot platform he could read the big sign: HARVEY HOUSE—Restaurant & Hotel." It filled the entire facade of the newly painted building.

A wide veranda extended across the entire front of the two-story structure, and the bright light of acetylene lamps shone through screened double doors. Longarm went inside and looked around. Only three or four of the dozen tables were occupied. A long counter stretched across the back of the room, half a dozen of its stools filled.

Several young women wearing crisply starched white dresses and pert triangular white stand-up headbands trimmed with black braid were bustling around in the big room. One of them came to greet Longarm. He noticed that her headdress and the breast of her dress were embroidered with the words "Harvey House," and in addition the dress bore the name "Edna."

"Would you prefer a table or the counter, sir?" she asked.

"Well, now, that depends. I'm looking for a fellow named George Forbes. He's supposed to be in here having supper. Maybe you can show me where he's sitting."

"Oh, of course. Mr. Forbes is one of our regulars," the girl said. She glanced around the room quickly and turned back to Longarm, pointing. "That's him, at the table in the back right-hand corner."

"Thank you kindly," Longarm nodded, touching his hat-brim. He started toward the table she'd indicated.

"Will you be wanting to order?" the waitress asked. "If you do, I'll be right with you."

Longarm suddenly realized how hungry he was. Lunch had been a pair of tamales from the basket of a trackside vendor at one of the little towns where the accommodation train had stopped late in the morning.

"Now, that's a real good idea," he replied. He looked at the name embroidered on her dress. "Sure, Edna. Come get my order whenever you're ready. And if your barroom's got some good Maryland rye, I'd like a little tot before supper."

"I'm sorry, sir," the girl told him. "Mr. Harvey doesn't allow liquor in his places."

"Now, that plumb slipped my mind," Longarm smiled. "I oughta have remembered that from the time I stayed at the

Harvey House in Gallup. I'll settle for hot coffee, if you'll be so kind as to bring me a cup."

"Certainly, sir. And I'll take your order then."

Longarm walked over to the table the waitress had pointed out and stopped beside it.

"You be George Forbes?" he asked.

"Yes. What can I do for you?"

"My name's Long, Mr. Forbes. Deputy U. S. marshal outa the Denver office. Chief Marshal Higgins up in Santa Fe asked my chief to send me here to see if I can help you find them bonds and stuff that's missing, and I—"

"Just a minute, Marshal Long," Forbes broke in. "I'm not the one you want to talk to about that. You need to see the district superintendent, Frank Carstow. You'll find him in his office at the depot."

"Let me finish what I begun telling you, Mr. Forbes," Longarm replied. "I got some bad news for you. Carstow's dead."

"Dead!" Forbes exclaimed. "How could he be? Why, he was in good health when I left him to come over here for supper!"

"He was shot," Longarm said flatly. "Murdered. Somebody hiding out in your yards put a bullet through his head. Shot right through a window."

"That's terrible!" Forbes said, shaking his head. "Why would anyone want to kill Frank?"

"I got some ideas about that," Longarm said. He stopped as he saw the waitress approaching, then went on, "I better sit down with you, if you don't mind. I told that girl to come get my supper order. Figured it'd save time if we talked while I eat; I didn't get much on the way here on your accommodation."

"Sit down, of course," Forbes nodded. "But shouldn't I be getting back to the depot? There'll be a lot of details—"

"They'll wait," Longarm told him, pulling out a chair and settling into it. "I told your stationmaster what happened. He's staying to keep an eye on things."

"Here's your coffee, sir, and if you're ready to order, sir," the waitress said, placing a cup of steaming coffee in front of Longarm and offering him a menu card. "I'm sure you'll find something you'll like on the menu."

Longarm pushed the card aside and replied, "I don't need that. All I want is a fried steak and some fried potatoes."

"Of course. I'll bring your order right away."

After the waitress moved away, Longarm turned back to Forbes and picked up their interrupted conversation, saying, "I figure your boss getting killed is tied in with them missing bonds. Wouldn't you think so?"

"I suppose," Forbes agreed. "Even if I can't see how. You understand, Marshal Long, neither Frank nor I ever saw those bonds. It's hard for me to make any connection, but you'd know more about such things than I do."

Even before sitting down at the table, Longarm had been studying Forbes. The assistant superintendent was a thin man, his long face ending in a protruding jaw, his nose as sharp-edged as a hatchet. His high brow bore the lines of one who wore a habitual frown, and his dark eyes appeared a trifle too big for his face. Longarm guessed him to be a bit short of forty.

Longarm asked, "You and Carstow ain't been having trouble with the townfolks, have you? Or the railroad help?"

Forbes shook his head. "No. Oh, there's always a certain amount of trouble in a town like this, because the people who settled it are mostly riffraff left over from the Hell-on-Wheels days. They just stopped here when we got orders from the main office in Chicago to quit building."

"How long ago was that?"

"Two, almost three years ago. You see, Marshal Long, the Santa Fe's route was surveyed right after the negotiations with the SP were settled. The original plan was to build the main line direct to California."

Longarm nodded. "I know a little bit about that. I was on a case up at Albuquerque when the rails was being laid to Gallup and on beyond."

"That was before my time down here," Forbes said. "But when the SP decided to withdraw from the agreement they'd made to let Santa Fe tracks run south of the Rockies, someone in our head office figured out that we could build a spur that would loop southeast from Albuquerque up through Tucson and connect with the main line in the middle of Arizona."

"But it only got this far?"

"That's about the size of it," Forbes said. "Everything stopped here, partly because it's one of the few places along the spur where there's water. But the real reason was that so much construction material had been stockpiled here. It was cheaper to let it stay with a small crew to look after it than to ship it back. And I'm sure the head office intends to push the spur on into Arizona Territory, the way it was planned originally."

"I guess that'd make sense," Longarm nodded. "And that's how the town came to be built? The folks that'd been following the construction gangs stopped here, too?"

"Well, they didn't have much of anywhere else to go," Forbes replied. "I'd say about half of them are drifters who decided to settle here until we start pushing rail again. Then they'll go back to the life they lived before."

"Most of them people are pretty cross-grained, from what I seen of 'em," Longarm commented. "I'm sorta surprised they ain't given you a bad time."

"They keep pretty much to themselves," Forbes said. "Some of them are men from our old construction gangs who took up land and stayed to start farms or small cattle ranches. And we haven't had too much trouble. Oh, there've been some thefts, material from the yards, and now and then a parcel or a suitcase from the baggage room at the depot, but that's about all."

"You and Carstow was left here to keep an eye on things, then, when the construction was shut down?"

"Yes," Forbes replied. "Frank is—was, I guess I ought to say—a surveyor as well as an engineer. He's been spending a good deal of his time surveying on west, and I've been in charge of the materials yard."

Longarm nodded. He said, "Well, you ought to know about the town, then. Did—" He stopped as the waitress returned with his supper, and the sight of his steak and potatoes reminded him how hungry he was. He told Forbes, "I'm going to start eating while this meat's still hot. Suppose you just go on and tell me what you know about them missing bonds."

"I don't imagine I know any more than you do, Marshal," the Santa Fe man said. "Nobody here even knew those bonds were being sent until they turned up missing."

Longarm swallowed the bite of steak he was chewing before

he asked, "You mean your head office in Chicago didn't tell you they was on the way?"

Forbes shook his head. "Chicago notified us there was a special shipment coming, and that it was to be held unopened until we got further instructions. That was all."

"I guess you took special care of it, then?"

"Marshal Long, as I just said, we didn't have any orders except to hold the shipment. And that's exactly what we did."

"Where'd you hold it? In that car Carstow used for his office and bedroom?"

"No. In the baggage room at the depot."

Without trying to mask the suspicion in his voice, Longarm asked, "You mean to tell me you didn't pay any attention to the wire you'd got from your head office?"

Forbes did not reply for a moment, and when he did it was obvious that he was keeping his voice in tight control. He said, "Let me tell you exactly what happened, Marshal. Maybe then you can understand the situation better."

"Go ahead," Longarm nodded. "I'll eat while you talk."

"You came in one the accommodation today," Forbes began. "I guess you noticed that it started back to Albuquerque as soon as the engineer could turn his locomotive on the shunt siding."

"I wasn't paying all that much mind to the train," Longarm replied. "Except I noticed it wasn't there after I'd come outa Carstow's car."

"That's the way the accommodation operates," Forbes went on. "A fast turnaround and back to Albuquerque. Now, I suppose you know that the suitcase with the bonds in it was brought here from Chicago by a man from the Pinkerton Detective Agency?"

"So I was told," Longarm nodded.

"Well, the Pinkerton man's job was finished when he handed the suitcase over to us here in Deming. He was anxious to catch the accommodation back, so he just delivered the suitcase to the stationmaster and left."

"Seems to me the stationmaster'd have told you or Carstow that it'd got there," Longarm frowned.

"He tried to. He knew it was the special shipment we'd

58

been told to expect, so he brought it right over to Carstow's office. It just happened that neither Carstow nor I was there at the moment, so he took the suitcase back to the depot, where he could keep an eye on it."

"I'd say he didn't do too good a job of watching," Longarm observed. "Ain't you got a safe in the depot?"

"Of course. But the safe's not big enough to hold a suitcase. So the stationmaster put it in the baggage room."

"When did you find out it'd turned up missing?"

"Not until he looked for it when Carstow had gotten back."

"How long was that?"

"Oh, a matter of a couple of hours," Forbes replied.

"And then it wasn't there?"

"There wasn't a sign of it."

"I imagine you looked everyplace?"

"Certainly we did!" Forbes said, his voice sharp. "We searched the depot and baggage room and even Carstow's car. And I'm sure you know the rest of it."

"Not exactly," Longarm answered. "I guess you notified the folks in your head office it was missing?"

"By the time we'd given up hope of finding it, the Chicago office was closed. We did the next best thing. We wired the Santa Fe's special agent's office at the Chicago Union Station. That was about eight o'clock in the evening. And just before midnight, all hell broke loose."

"You mean you men had a fracas here?"

"Not here, Marshal. In Chicago. You see, we only keep the telegraph wire open to Albuquerque while the accommodation train's on the track. As soon as it's reported in at Albuquerque we close the depot. That's usually about midnight. We were just getting ready to close the wire when a message came through from Chicago that Carstow and I were to stay by the instrument, which we did. That's when the fur started flying."

"I get the idea the railroad special agent in Chicago had told your bosses about them bonds disappearing by then," Longarm remarked. "And I can see why they'd be a mite upset."

"Upset is too mild a word," Forbes replied. "They were in a red-hot stew. Why, I suppose we had everybody except Cyrus Holliday himself on that wire before the night was over."

"And that was when you and Carstow found out what was in the suitcase?"

Forbes nodded. "For the first time. And I'll tell you this for a fact, Marshal Long: I never want to go through a night like that again!"

"I can see it'd be uncomfortable," Longarm agreed. "And I guess you've looked all over for the suitcase since then?"

"It's been almost two weeks since the suitcase disappeared, and we haven't stopped looking for a minute."

"You called in the local law, I imagine?"

"That was the first thing we did. We had every man from the Santa Fe's special agent force in Albuquerque here until they had to go back to their regular routine jobs. That was when we asked the chief U. S. marshal in Santa Fe for help. I guess that brings us up to date."

Longarm had finished eating by now. He pushed his empty plate aside and said, "It's about time I got to work, then."

Forbes shook his head. "I don't know, Marshal. It's been more than two weeks since those bonds disappeared. I don't want to discourage you, but I'm afraid you'll just be wasting your time. As far as I can see, those bonds are gone forever."

Chapter 7

Longarm looked at Forbes for a moment. Then he said quietly, "Maybe I don't give up as easy as you do, Mr. Forbes. Now, I just got to Deming a little while ago, and so far all I know about this case is what somebody else has told me. I don't like to sound like I'm bragging, but I don't let up on a case till I close it. And I sure don't plan to close this one till I've found them bonds."

"Oh, of course!" Forbes said hastily. "And whatever I can do to help—"

"Don't worry, if I need your help I'll sure let you know," Longarm assured the Santa Fe man. "There's one thing I'd like to ask you before I start noseying around, though. Does your local lawman feel like you do about them bonds being gone for good?"

"Buck Tyler? The town marshal?"

"I ain't heard his name before, but go ahead and tell me about him."

"Well . . ." Forbes hesitated a moment before going on, then said, "Maybe you ought to ask somebody else that question, Marshal Long. I'm afraid I'm prejudiced."

"It sounds to me like you and him ain't on very good terms," Longarm observed.

"That's a polite way to put it," Forbes said with a sour little smile.

"I take it you've had some run-ins?"

"Nothing serious," Forbes replied quickly. "We haven't had any head-to-head collisions. The thing is, Tyler used to be on the Santa Fe's railroad police force. He made a few mistakes, and I had the job of firing him."

"What kind of mistakes?"

Forbes countered Longarm's questions with one of his own.

"Have you ever seen a railhead construction camp when track-laying was in full swing, Marshal?"

"Sure. I had a case a few years back at the Santa Fe railhead when they was building west from Albuquerque. I guess they're all pretty much the same, riffraff from Hell-on-Wheels keeping things stirred up, fights and petty thievery going on all the time."

"That's right," Forbes agreed. "Tyler didn't seem to be able to keep construction materials and tools from disappearing, and he spent too much time in the gambling houses and saloons to suit me. Mr. Carstow and I agreed he was neglecting his job, and it was my job to fire him. Tyler doesn't like me very much because of that."

"I can see where he wouldn't have much use for you or the Santa Fe," Longarm nodded. "I guess he didn't put himself out to help when you told him the suitcase was missing?"

"Tyler claimed that it wasn't his problem. He said that the suitcase disappeared from Santa Fe property, and it was up to our railroad police to find it."

"He didn't do anything at all about it, then?"

"Oh, he talked to the stationmaster, and looked around the depot and baggage room, but his effort stopped there," Forbes replied. "He got very angry when I told him he was wasting his time, because both Mr. Carstow and I had questioned the stationmaster and searched the baggage room ourselves."

"You and him had an argument, then?"

"Perhaps I'm making it sound worse than it was, Marshal. We didn't argue or quarrel. Tyler just froze up and walked away. I haven't seen him since then."

Longarm sat silently for a moment, then said, "Well, this killing's his case, so I'll have to report it to him."

"Just don't expect him to do much, Marshal Long," Forbes said. "To be frank, I don't think that Tyler could help you much on this kind of an ambush killing even if he wanted to, which I'm sure he doesn't."

"I'll have to talk to him just the same. I guess you know us U. S. marshals has got rules to go by, just like your railroad does," Longarm said. "But before I go to see him, I better get me a room here at the Harvey House. It's close to the yards and not too far from the middle of town."

Shaking his head, Forbes said, "I'm afraid you're not going to be able to stay here, Marshal."

"You mean it's full up?"

"I mean that this restaurant is the only part of the Harvey House that's finished," Forbes explained. "You see, when Mr. Harvey started building this place, the Santa Fe hadn't stopped construction on the spur. When we closed down our job, he decided not to open the hotel until the spur's finished. Without any through traffic on the railroad, there simply wouldn't have been any point in completing it."

"I'll just have to go someplace else, then."

"That's right. Now, unless you object to sleeping in a dead man's bed, Mr. Carstow's car won't be in use any more. You're welcome to stay in it. I'd invite you to stay with me, but my car's only got one bunk in it."

"Well, I sure can't stay in Carstow's car tonight," Longarm frowned. "Your friend Tyler's going to want to come look at it, and after that I guess it'll be up to you to see about having the undertaker move the body."

"You'd better stay at the hotel in town tonight, then," Forbes suggested. "It's pretty run-down, but I'm sure you can stand it for one night. You can move into Mr. Carstow's car in the morning."

"That's the best thing to do, I guess," Longarm agreed. "I'll just walk back to the depot with you and pick up my gear. Then when I go to town to tell Tyler what's happened, I can stop at the hotel and get fixed up with a room."

"You'll be going back to the depot with me after all, then," Forbes said, pushing back his chair and standing up.

Longarm rose also. As he stepped up to join Forbes, one of the waitresses came up.

"Excuse me, Mr. Forbes," she said. "I'm sorry to break into your conversation, but I saw you gentlemen getting ready to leave. Edna's gone off duty, but she asked me to give you your dinner checks."

"Of course," Forbes replied, taking the dinner ticket she handed him. "Thank you, Anita."

"Thank you, Mr. Forbes," she replied, turning to Longarm.

"And here's yours, sir."

"Thanks," Longarm said, extending his hand.

"You're very welcome, sir." She smiled, turning away.

As Longarm followed Forbes to the cashier's station, he raised the dinner ticket to look at the amount. The stiff ticket was folded double and the tiny slip of thin paper that had been hidden in the fold almost fell to the floor, but he managed to grab it in time. When he held the paper up, he saw something had been written on it, only a few words, which he read at a glance while he waited for Forbes to get his change.

In small, clear script the note read: *Meet me back door. Five minutes. Alone. Important.*

Having been given the note by the Harvey girl, Longarm assumed she'd written it. Keeping his face expressionless, he refolded the paper. Holding it cupped in his palm, he put his hand in his pocket and left the note there when he brought out the money to pay his supper check. He followed Forbes outside.

As Longarm joined him, Forbes said, "When that Harvey girl interrupted us, I was just about to say that as little as I like our town marshal, I suppose I'll have to work with him." He hesitated for a moment, then added hopefully, "Unless you'd consider Mr. Carstow's murder part of your case. Then you cold investigate it yourself, Marshal Long."

"I'm sorry, but I can't do that," Longarm replied. "The murder's a local case, so whether I like it or not, I'll have to turn it over to your town marshal. Which don't mean I won't keep working on it myself in private."

"Tyler won't be very happy about that," Forbes said. "And he certainly won't be cooperative. As I said, he's been angry with me and the Santa Fe since I handed him his walking papers."

"I'll go light in mentioning your name when I talk to him," Longarm said. He'd seen the answer to his problem of meeting the Harvey House waitress when Forbes made his suggestion. He went on, "I'll tell you what, Mr. Forbes. Instead of going back to the depot with you, I'll go into town and tell the marshal about Mr. Carstow. Then I'll come back with him and stay around until he's done whatever work he'll have to take care of. That way you might not even have to talk to him."

"If you'd do that, I'll certainly appreciate it, Marshal Long," Forbes said. "I'll walk on over to the depot, then, and wait for you to come back with Tyler."

"Don't worry if I don't get back right away," Longarm told Forbes. "I'll stop at the hotel in town and get me a room for tonight. And it might take me a few minutes to put Tyler in the right frame of mind."

"If I'm not at the depot, I'll be in my own car," Forbes said. "It's just down the siding from Carstow's."

"I'll try not to disturb you till after I've talked to Tyler and got rid of him," Longarm said. "It might be pretty late."

"Don't worry about the time," Forbes replied. "The way it looks now, I'm not going to get much sleep tonight. Don't hesitate to come down to my car, Marshal Long, no matter how late it is when you and Tyler get through."

Forbes turned and started for the depot. Longarm watched him disappear in the gloom before walking around to the rear of the Harvey House. There was no one waiting, and he took out a cheroot and lighted it. He'd just gotten the long, slim cigar drawing satisfactorily when he saw the waitress come around the opposite corner of the building, her white uniform ghostly in the gloom. Longarm walked to meet her.

"I'm sorry if I kept you waiting, Marshal Long," she said as he stopped. "I couldn't get out of the dining room as soon as I'd planned, because I had to finish serving Edna's tables."

"I just got here a minute ago myself," Longarm replied. "Now maybe you better tell me what's on your mind."

Instead of answering directly, she went on, "I'm sure you noticed my first name on my uniform when I gave you the check. My full name's Anita Bradley, and I work for Allan Pinkerton."

"And how'd you come to know who I am?" Longarm asked. He made no effort to hide the skepticism in his voice.

"Because when I changed trains at Albuquerque on the way here there was a telegram waiting for me from our Chicago office. It said you were going to be assigned to this case, and suggested that you might be willing for us to work together."

"Not meaning to doubt your word, Miss Bradley, but I guess you got some way of proving what you just told me?" Longarm asked.

"Of course I have! Will my Pinkerton badge and identification card satisfy you?"

"They'd go a long way toward easing my mind," Longarm admitted.

Anita Bradley bent down, pulled up her ankle-length skirt, and took a thin wallet from the top of one of her high-button shoes. As she handed the wallet to Longarm she said, "If this isn't enough to satisfy you, Marshal, I can show you the telegram I got from the Chicago office. It's in my room."

Longarm puffed hard on his cigar and by holding its glowing coal close to the badge he was able to see the familiar Pinkerton name and to make out the detective agency's well-known open-eye insignia on the identification card.

"Looks like you're who you say you are," he told her, returning the wallet. "When did you get here, Miss Bradley?"

"Just over a week ago."

"Your boss sure didn't waste any time. I got a hunch he knew I was going to draw this assignment even before I did."

"Well, Mr. Pinkerton has a lot of good friends in Washington, Marshal. And he does move very fast, especially on a case where one of our operatives has made a mistake."

"Forbes told me about that mixup. The Pinkerton man just left the suitcase at the depot instead of finding Mr. Carstow and delivering it to him."

Anita nodded. "You can imagine what happened when the news got back to Chicago that our man hadn't done what he was supposed to. Within twenty-four hours, Mr. Pinkerton had arranged my cover job at the Harvey House—luckily, Mr. Fred Harvey was in Chicago at that time—and I left at once."

"I'd heard a while back that Pinkerton's had hired a lady detective, but this is the first time I ever run into one."

Longarm's eyes had adjusted to the darkness now and he could see that Anita Bradley had an attractive but not extraordinarily pretty face. She was neither beautiful nor ugly; her features were regular, and she had dark hair that was almost hidden by the peak of her Harvey House headband. The long, full-cut waitress uniform also hid the details of her figure. All he could tell was that she was tall and slender.

She said, "Oh, I'm not Pinkerton's only female operative. There are two more in the Chicago office and another in our Washington office."

"Well, now that we've got together, maybe you'd like to tell me what's on you mind, Miss Bradley," Longarm suggested. "You said in your note it was important for me to meet you."

"Please, Marshal Long, call me Anita, or, better yet, Nita," she said.

"Why, sure. And, seeing as we're going to be partners in a way, I got a sorta nickname I answer to better'n anything else."

"Yes, I've heard it. Longarm. You're quite well-known to us in the agency, if you aren't already aware of that."

"Well, I didn't know it, but I've come across more'n one Pinkerton man on cases I've worked." Longarm took a final puff on his cigar and tossed the butt aside. "Now, what did you want to tell me about this case, Nita?"

"If you're asking for facts, I'm sure I don't have any that you don't already know," Anita replied. "And I can't stay off my job long enough for us to compare notes. All I really wanted to do was tell you I'm here and offer to work with you."

"You know, I think that's a prime idea," Longarm agreed. "You heard the Santa Fe superintendent was murdered, I guess?"

"I overheard someone say Frank Carstow had been killed, but I didn't get any of the details."

Longarm filled Anita in on the bare facts that he knew, and added, "I'm on my way now to tell the town marshal about the killing. You've run into Buck Tyler, ain't you?"

"I've seen him a time or two, but he doesn't know what my real job is here," she replied. "Mr. Carstow knew, but I'm sure he didn't pass the information on to Mr. Forbes. And the head office hasn't authorized me to tell anybody except you that I'm on the job."

"Then the town marshal won't know, either?"

"Of course not. But, if you're interested in exchanging information with me, they've given me permission to."

"I ain't got anything to pass on right now," Longarm said. "But I will have tomorrow." Then he recalled what Anita had said a moment earlier and went on, "You said you heard somebody talking about Carstow getting killed. I'd bet dollars to doughnuts that all the girls in a place like the Harvey House hear a lot of things the customers are talking about, don't they?"

"We certainly do! Being a waitress is almost as good as being invisible."

"How many of you work in the Harvey House here?"

"There are eight of us, counting me. Right now I'm on the morning shift with Edna and Josie and Mary. Coretta, Blossom, Janet, and Susan work the night shift, and two of us from each shift have overlapping hours to handle the noon and supper rush."

"I guess you swap gossip? Women mostly do."

"So do men, Longarm," Anita said quickly. "You'd be surprised at some of the things I overhear, waiting on tables."

"Maybe I would, at that. But it takes a lot to surprise me. I can see where you might pick up some information that'd help close out this case."

"I haven't heard anything like that so far," Anita said. "But I've started asking the other girls questions about the gossip they pick up. I've learned a lot of interesting things, but so far nothing useful about this case. You're right, though, we need to get together and exchange information."

"Fine," Longarm agreed. "Now all we need to do is figure out where and when we can get together."

"I can't be of much help with that," she told him. "Right now, we're all sleeping in a big room on the upper floor. It was supposed to be a banquet room, and they turned it into a kind of dormitory for the waitresses. I'm sure you can imagine what it's like."

"How about someplace else on that upper floor?"

Anita shook her head. "The only stairway that was completed when they stopped construction goes to our sleeping room from the kitchen. And no men are allowed to use it."

"We'll have to meet where I'll be staying, then," Longarm told her. "I'll be at the hotel in town tonight, but tomorrow I'm going to move into that railroad coach the Santa Fe superintendent was using. It oughta be private enough."

"That sounds good," Anita nodded. "If I have anything I'd like to pass on, I can give you a note like I did just now, and we can meet and talk."

"Let's leave it at that, then," Longarm nodded. "Now you got to get back inside, and I got to go tell Buck Tyler that he's got a murder case on his hands."

Longarm watched Nita vanish around the corner of the building, then turned and started walking thoughtfully toward the lights of Deming's main street.

Chapter 8

With a final look around the bare little room he'd taken at the Deming Hotel, Longarm went down the stairs to the lower floor and sauntered out into the street. He stood in front of the hotel and lighted a cheroot while he looked over the town.

Complete darkness had settled in by now, and the air was beginning to grow cool. Along Deming's main—and only—street, lights spilled out of open doors of the town's handful of stores and around the batwings of the much more numerous saloons, the harsh blue-white glow of acetylene lights mingling with the softer yellow brightness of coal-oil lamps. Beyond the street the mellow golden glow of coal-oil lamps shone from the windows of the houses dotted on the rising ground that stretched away from the town.

Longarm had to try two saloons before he found one that had rye whiskey. Even at the third saloon he was not offered Maryland rye, but had to settle for a tot of Pennsylvania barrel whiskey, which he still judged better than the sweetish bourbon that cloyed his palate. He tossed off the drink quickly and lighted a fresh cigar as he walked on down to the end of the street and the small, square, unpainted wooden building that over its half-open door bore the sign TOWN MARSHAL.

Stopping in the doorway, Longarm peered inside. A burly man wearing duck jeans and a leather vest was sitting at a rolltop desk. He was bending forward, his back to the door, his attention fixed on a sheaf of papers that he was shuffling, and apparently had not heard Longarm's approaching footsteps grating across the gravelled ground.

Longarm took in the building's interior with a single quick glance. It was as bare of paint or decoration as the outside. By the light of the coal-oil lamp that stood on top of the rolltop desk he saw the bars of three narrow cells. They were each barely wide enough to accommodate a bunk, and took up the entire rear end of the structure.

The smell peculiar to jails hung in the air of the little room, but none of the cells was occupied, though one of them was piled high with a clutter of miscellaneous boxes and bulging gunny sacks. The desk at which the occupant of the office sat filled most of the wall on one side, and on the opposite side a long bench stretched between the front wall and the cells.

Longarm cleared his throat and the man at the desk swivelled to look at him. He asked, "You looking for somebody, friend?"

His voice was anything but friendly. Longarm saw the star pinned on his vest and was sure he'd found the man he was looking for. He also was sure of what his instinct told him when he heard the few words the town marshal had spoken: that Tyler was one of the overbearing, self-important type of lawmen for whom Longarm had little regard.

"I sure am," Longarm replied, stepping through the door and stopping before he reached the desk. "I'm looking for the town marshal, Buck Tyler."

"Well, you don't have to look no more. You found him. I'm Tyler."

"My name's Long, Custis Long." Longarm's voice was as cold as Tyler's. "Deputy U. S. marshal, outa the Denver office."

"Long?" Tyler frowned, scratching the day-old bristles on his underslung bulldog's jaw as he scanned Longarm from hat to boot soles. He went on with a gathering frown, "A federal marshal. Now, wait a minute! You wouldn't be the one they call Longarm, would you?"

"Some folks call me that," Longarm admitted.

"I've heard about you," Tyler nodded, "and from what I hear, you close more cases with a bullet than you do in court."

"Well, now, when an outlaw I'm sent to bring in starts to shoot at me, I ain't a bit bashful about shooting back."

"That's as may be," Tyler said. "But I can't recall any federal business we've got that'd bring you to Deming. If you didn't drop in just to make a friendly call, suppose you tell me what's on your mind."

Longarm's respect for Tyler had plummeted still lower during their brief exchange, but he kept his voice level as he replied, "Why, I figured you'd tumble to that right off, because you turned down the case that I was sent here to handle."

"Oh, hell!" Tyler groaned. "I might've known it. Them damn pen-pushers that works for the Santa Fe pulled enough strings to get you sent here about that suitcase they claim somebody stole."

"Well, you're about half right," Longarm replied. "The chief marshal here in New Mexico Territory got me detached from Denver, so I'd say some strings got pulled. But until I find out different, I don't doubt their word about it being stolen."

"Now, look here, Long!" Tyler bristled. "That damn suitcase was likely lost someplace along the Santa Fe's own tracks, someplace between here and Chicago. It looks to me like—"

"Hold on, Tyler!" Longarm snapped, his patience at an end. "I didn't come in here to talk about my case any more'n I did to visit. I come to report a murder."

Tyler's brows knitted again as he gazed coldly at Longarm. Then he said, "You must've got to town on today's train, and it only pulled out something like three hours ago. Ain't you starting to kill people pretty fast?"

Longarm stifled the hot, angry retort that rose to his lips at Tyler's implied accusation. Instead he said coldly, "Don't go putting words in my mouth, Tyler. I never said I killed anybody, and just to keep things straight between us, I ain't had my gun outa my holster since I got here."

"What's this murder you're talking about, then?"

"When I went to tell the Santa Fe superintendent I'd got to town, I found him dead."

"Frank Carstow?" Tyler broke in with a frown. "I seen him on the street about noon today. What happened to him?"

"As near as I can tell, he was shot in the head by a sniper who was outside of that railroad car he lives in."

"How long ago did you find him?"

"A couple of hours ago, maybe a little bit more. His body was cold, so I figure he was shot sometime right after noon."

"You said he was shot by a sniper from outside his car. How the hell do you know?"

"Because the bullet that killed him was fired through the

72

window. Carstow'd been setting right by it, and the pane was busted. If that ain't enough to satisfy you, I found the slug dug into the wall across from where he'd been sitting. It was up close to the ceiling, so whoever pulled the trigger must've been laying on the ground shooting up through the window. Seems to me you oughta be able to figure that out for yourself."

"Don't get feisty with me now, Long!" Tyler grated. Then he frowned and went on in a milder tone, "It's dark now, and if you got in on the accommodation train you must've found that body four or five hours ago. How come you didn't report it sooner?"

"I stopped and had a bite of supper," Longarm answered. He slid a cigar from his pocket and took his time about lighting it. "I didn't see any need to hurry. Carstow was dead; he wasn't about to go anyplace."

"Did you tell anybody else about finding him?"

"I had to report the killing to the stationmaster and ask him to keep an eye on things. When I told him I was coming here to tell you, he said the assistant superintendent was having supper at the Harvey House, and he asked me to stop there and tell him about Carstow."

"That'd be George Forbes?" Tyler broke in. When Longarm nodded, the town marshal asked, "Did you tell him, then?"

"Why, sure. And, as long as I was there, I had a bite of supper, like I just said."

"You sure you didn't waste a lot of time prowling around the Santa Fe yards looking for the killer, maybe spooking him off?" Tyler asked.

"Like I told you a minute ago, Carstow's body was cold. I didn't figure the fellow that had shot him was waiting around for somebody to find him. Besides, a local murder's in your jurisdiction, not mine."

"Something else I've heard about you, Long, is that you don't pay much attention to rules. How come you're being so particular about whose jurisdiction applies on this killing?"

"I got enough to do, working on the case I was sent here for. Of course, if you figure you're gonna need some help—"

"When I need your help on a case of mine, it'll be the day hell freezes over!" Tyler growled.

"Well, I've done what I come for, Tyler," Longarm said. "I told you all I know, and since you say you don't need no help, I'll go on about my own case."

Longarm turned to leave, then turned back and dug into his vest pocket to take out the bullet he'd pried from the wall of the Santa Fe superintendent's office.

"This is the slug that killed Carstow," he said, tossing the bullet on Tyler's desk. "In case you ain't up to recognizing the barrel-land spacing, it's a .45-.70 and it was fired outa a Winchester."

Looking at the mushroom-shaped bit of the lead, Tyler snorted, "A hell of a lot of good that is! There's maybe two or three hundred .45-.70 Winchesters around Deming. Every son of a bitch and his brother carries one for a saddle gun! I do, so does my deputy, so does every farmer and sheep-herder you run into!"

"Then it's up to you to find which of them sons of bitches or his brother it was that pulled the trigger of the Winchester this slug came out of, ain't it?" Longarm retorted.

He turned away from Tyler and started toward the door, but before he reached it there was a shuffling of feet on the gravel outside and two men came in. One of them had a gunbelt on, and Longarm placed him as Tyler's deputy even before he saw the star pinned on his vest.

Under the broken bill of the weather-worn cloth cap worn by the other man Longarm could see a dirt-stained face grizzled by a three-day beard. He placed the man as being in his forties. He was blinking colorless eyes, his head swivelling from side to side. He had on a tattered knee-length overcoat and the legs of the trousers visible below its fringed bottom were ragged and dirt-stained. The cap was his most outstanding item of apparel. It was made of black and white checked wool fabric and even in its present dilapidated state Longarm could see that originally it had been a very expensive piece of headgear.

Before either of the new arrivals could speak, Tyler burst out, "Why in hell did you bring that bum back here, Peters? I told you to let him eat some supper and then kick him out of town!"

"Well, he just wanted to thank you for his supper, Buck," Peters replied. "I figured it'd be easier to let him do that than to fight him all the way out to the town limits."

Longarm's ears pricked up at the deputy's words. Tyler hadn't struck him as being a man who'd buy a hobo a meal before banishing him. He stepped back against the wall where he would be as inconspicuous as possible.

"When I tell you to do something, I want you to do it!" Tyler went on. "Now get him outa my sight!"

"Don't go blaming your deppity, Marshal!" the hobo said quickly. "It was my fault. Like he said, I just wanted to thank you for being so nice to me."

"All right!" Tyler snapped. "You've thanked me, so go on and get the hell outa here. And from now on steer clear of Deming, like you promised me you would!"

"Bones Jones don't forget a man that's done him a favor, Marshal," the hobo said. "You don't hafta worry. Bones Jones keeps his promises, too. I ain't going to come back here, no siree! You can sure count on that!"

"You better not come back!" Tyler snarled. "You know what you'll get if you do!"

"Sure, sure," Bones Jones replied. He turned to the deputy and went on, "I'll go along nice and quiet now, just like I promised. And I won't be bothering you no more."

"See that you don't, then!" Tyler said. "Now get the hell outa my sight."

Still puzzled, Longarm let the deputy and the hobo pass him before turning to go out himself. He'd almost reached the door when Tyler called to him.

"Wait a minute, Long!" the marshal said. When Longarm turned to face him, Tyler went on gruffly, "Don't get the idea I'm a soft touch, just because I let a hobo have a decent meal."

"I wasn't getting no ideas at all," Longarm shrugged. "I'd imagine you got a lot of men just like that one passing through."

"And it's my job to keep 'em moving," Tyler nodded. "It ain't the best part." He hesitated, then added, "You might not believe this, Long, but there was a time when I was down on my luck, and I looked and smelled just like old Bones Jones does. I know what that kind of life is like, and I always let 'em get a good feed before I do what my job calls for me to do, and roust 'em outa town."

Longarm's expression had not changed as he listened to the marshal's glib explanation. He said, "Now that's real generous of you, Tyler. I bet it makes you feel good all over to be so nice to them poor devils. Likely that's why you waited till it got dark to start him on his way."

"I've had enough of your snide talk, Long!" Tyler snapped. "You made your report, and I'm in charge now. Suppose you just go on back to the depot, and try to keep out from under my feet the rest of the time you're in Deming."

"That'll be a real pleasure," Longarm replied levelly. He turned and left the office and strolled back toward the center of town.

During the time he'd spent in Tyler's office, most of the stores had closed, but the saloons were still lighted and doing business and the streets were far from being deserted. Most of the men Longarm passed were roughly dressed, and he tagged them mentally as being the Hell-on-Wheels denizens who'd decided to wait in Deming until the Santa Fe started laying rails again.

He reached the hotel and started to go inside when the light spilling out around the batwings of the saloon across the street caught his eye and reminded him that when he'd looked in earlier the saloon had been so crowded that he hadn't gone in. The swinging doors also reminded him that he hadn't yet had his nightcap, nor did he have his customary bottle of Tom Moore in his room.

Longarm crossed the street and pushed through the swinging doors. As early as the hour was, the saloon was empty now except for two customers at the bar and a solitary drinker at a table in the back corner. He walked past the two men who were busy with some discussion of their own and stopped at the rear of the bar.

"What's your pleasure, friend?" the barkeep asked, making the traditional swipe with his towel across the mahogany in front of Longarm.

Dropping a silver cartwheel on the bar, Longarm replied, "Rye. Tom Moore's my first choice, if you got some."

"You got expensive taste, I see," the barkeep said with a low whistle.

Longarm's temper was still a bit frayed after his exchange with Tyler. He asked, "Are you saying the whiskey I enjoy is too high-priced for you to keep in stock?"

"Oh, I'm not making any snide remarks about your good taste, friend," the barkeep answered quickly. "And I'll be glad to oblige you with some Tom Moore. Just give me a minute to step in the back room and get a bottle."

"Hold on there," Longarm said as the man started to turn away. "I'll want my drink, but if you got another bottle of that Moore you can spare, I'll buy it off you."

"No trouble with that, either. I'll be right back."

After setting one bottle of the whiskey in front of Longarm, the barkeep busied himself opening the second and pulling its cork. As he filled Longarm's glass, he said, "Since the Santa Fe quit laying tracks we don't get many customers who appreciate a fine whiskey. I'd say you're new in town, since I haven't seen you in here before. Just passing through?"

"Oh, I'll likely be around a few days," Longarm answered, taking out a cigar and lighting it. He raised his glass and swallowed half the pungent liquor.

"Not much to do in Deming these days," the barkeep went on. "Things have sure changed here. The town's quieted down from the way it used to be."

"You'd be an old-timer, then," Longarm said after finishing his drink.

"Mister, I was here before this place was named Deming. It was Hell on Wheels then, moving along the Santa Fe while they pushed the tracks west."

"I can see why you'd find it a mite different now."

"It was sure different then," the barkeeper went on. "Hell on Wheels died when construction stopped. I never did put in with the riffraff, you understand. I was glad to see most of them go when everything stopped. It's picked up a little since then, but it's a lot tamer. I guess you've looked around?"

"Some," Longarm admitted. "Not all that much. I'd say you got the makings of a good town, though."

"Oh, sure. But I guess I still miss the way it was before. It was right wild then. Every saloon had games, and I ran the gambling in the biggest one. I get lonesome for that now, since the town council's outlawed it. Of course, if a man had a lot of time on his hands and wanted to sit in for a few hands of poker, or take a whirl at keno or faro, I imagine he could find a game, even if the town marshal keeps a lid on things."

"You're talking about Buck Tyler?" Longarm asked.

"That's right. Tyler keeps the games shut down tight," the barkeep replied. "If you knew him, you'd know he's tough as the sole of a brand-new boot."

"I wouldn't say I know him. I just met him a little while ago, and I had him tagged about like you do, a real tough one. Then he surprised me."

"Oh? How's that?"

"Why, I seen him buy a hobo a meal before he kicked him outa town."

"Are you sure we're talking about the same Buck Tyler?" the barkeep frowned. "Now, I've known Buck since before he was town marshal, and if there's one thing he hates and detests, it's hoboes and bums."

"All I can tell you is that I was in Tyler's office when this hobo come in to say thanks to him for being so nice."

"Oh, I don't question your word," the barkeep said hastily. "It just ain't like Buck to do a thing like that, is all." He looked closely at Longarm and went on, "You work for the Santa Fe, do you?"

"No. I just come in to give 'em a little help on something they been having trouble with."

"You're going to be around a while, I guess?"

"A while," Longarm nodded.

An idea had sprung full-grown into his mind, and he began elaborating on it as he tapped the rim of his glass to indicate he wanted a refill. While the barkeep was pouring, he slipped one hand into his trouser pocket and took out four of the gold double-eagles from his poker winnings in Denver. He dropped the coins on the bar beside the cartwheel and shoved one of them in the barkeep's direction.

"Take the price of my bottle and drinks outa one of them," he told the barkeep. "I ain't got any small change." When the man returned from the till with his change, Longarm went on, "I got the idea from what you said a minute ago that if a man wanted to set in on a poker game he wouldn't have much trouble finding one someplace outside the town limits."

"If he's really interested, I guess he might," the barkeep agreed. "Now, there's a hack stand next door, and one of the drivers is named Hank. If I was you, I'd go talk to him. You might mention I sent you over."

"Thanks, friend," Longarm nodded. Scooping up his change, he crossed the street and stopped at the hotel long enough to leave the bottle of Tom Moore in his room. As he placed the rye on the bureau, he looked at his image in the mirror.

One thing's for sure, old son, he told himself silently, *any place where a law's being broke there's bound to be crooks. They're like them birds of a feather, and that poker game's about the likeliest place to start looking for 'em. It oughta get your toe in the door, and if you ain't bright enough to shove your foot in and then your leg, then you better turn in your badge and start peddling peanuts.*

Chapter 9

Longarm peered out the window of the creaking, dilapidated hackney cab. For the past quarter of an hour since they'd left Deming it had been jolting over a road which was little more than two ruts meandering across the broken country. He looked back and saw that although the individual lights of Deming's outlying houses were no longer visible he could still see a glow of light beyond the horizon. Looking ahead he saw only blackness. He settled down as best he could, trying to find a spot on the seat where there was padding between him and the springs.

Before he'd found a more comfortable position the hackman reined in and leaned down from his seat to say through the open window, "We're here, mister."

Longarm leaned from the window and saw the outline of a half-soddie. No lights showed from the low-set structure.

"You sure this is the right place?" he asked.

"It's the place, all right. Just go knock on the door. If you want me to, I'll wait till Pete lets you in."

Longarm swung out of the hack. He told the driver, "That barkeep across from the hotel, who steered me to you, said there wasn't any charge to get out here, so I don't guess I owe you."

"Well, you don't, but if you'd feel like giving me a little tip, I wouldn't turn it down."

Longarm dug a quarter out of his pocket and handed it up to the hackie, then said, "Maybe you better tell me how in tunket I'm supposed to get back to town."

"Oh, Pete'll take care of that, just like he takes care of me for getting you here. On the nights when there's a game, he keeps a nag and a surrey out here to haul the players back."

"I guess that's all I need to know, then."

Longarm turned toward the soddie as the hackman flapped

the reins over his horse's back and the carriage creaked off. The outlines of the door were faintly visible, and he rapped. After a moment's wait the door swung open and an exceedingly fat man wearing farmer's bib overalls and a red and white checkered shirt was silhouetted in the light streaming from inside.

"Thought I heard that rig of Hank's a minute ago," the man said. "Come on in, mister. There ain't but one reason you're here, and the game ain't really got started good yet."

Ducking as he passed through the low-cut door, Longarm blinked in the lamplight. He took a cigar from his pocket and lighted it, blinking while his eyes adjusted to the lantern light, then took stock of his surroundings.

They were anything but plush. The sod house was like all those built by early settlers on the treeless and almost waterless prairie. Its back and side walls had been formed by excavating a square in one of the humps of the rolling ground and raising walls to a common level around the perimeter with bricks cut from the grassy topsoil, laid without mortar.

Longarm had seen many soddies, and his quick inspection told him that this was an old one, for the blocks of earth that formed its half-walls were cracked and beginning to crumble, showing the withered white roots of prairie grass here and there. The floor was packed earth, and the timbers that formed the low ceiling had curved downward over the years from the weight of the soil shovelled on top of them.

Window sashes had been framed to open on each side of the door, but they had been closed by boards nailed across them. In one corner of the ceiling the stub end of an unused stovepipe protruded into the low-ceilinged rectangular room, with a coal-oil lantern hanging from its end on a twisted wire.

There was no furniture except the bare essentials in the room. A table with its top covered by a horse blanket stood in the center; on it lay two decks of new playing cards, and behind it along the wall there were several empty chairs. Four men sat around it, stacks of silver dollars in front of them on the table. All of them were gazing at Longarm, and he gave each of them a quick look in turn, paying no attention to their stares.

None of the men looked remarkable. Two of them shared

one side of the table. One of them was youthful-looking and wore the rough clothing of a farmer. The other, in his forties, might have been a storekeeper or even a banker in his conservative blue suit. The man sitting at one end of the table was as thin as the man who'd greeted him was fat; he had a heavy, untrimmed moustache which was far too luxuriant for his narrow face, and wore a well-cut brown business suit. The fourth man's jaws and cheeks were hidden by a full beard, light brown verging on red, and he had thick eyebrows that were a shade darker than his beard; he was dressed in clothes that spoke of Mexico, *charro* pants and a vest of soft tan leather richly embroidered in silver.

While Longarm's gunmetal-blue eyes flicked quickly over the room and its occupants, the fat man who had opened the door stood silent. He closed the door now and turned to face Longarm.

"It ain't much to look at. It don't take lace curtains and a fancy rug for a poker game," he said, extending his hand. "I guess we better get acquainted before you join the game. My name's Pete, but most of my friends calls me Poker when I ain't holding better cards than they are. Then they're apt to call me something else, depending on how mad they get."

Longarm took the extended hand, saying, "I answer to Custis, Pete. The barkeep at the saloon across from the hotel said I'd find a good game out here."

"I figured as much," Pete nodded. He turned to the men at the table and said, "Boys, this is Custis," then went on, pointing as he spoke, "That's Sam in the red-checked shirt, and Bates is the name of the one setting next to him. That fellow at the other end of the table from me says his name's Brown, but on account of him going to sleep when he don't hold a good hand we just call him Shuteye. Now, that last man's a stranger, same as you are. He says his name's Ross, but if you was to call him Smith or Jones I'd imagine he'd answer."

"You didn't have no call to say that, Pete," Ross said without anger. "It ain't my fault, what I'm named."

"No harm intended, Ross," Pete said with a smile that showed a gold tooth in front of his mouth. He turned back to Longarm. "I better tell you the rules, Custis. Like you can see, we don't run to chips out here in the country. We play table stakes, and nobody checks the pot short. The ante's two dollars, the house gets a dollar of it. Low bet's a dollar and no limit on bets or raises. There's a joker in the deck, and it's the only card that's wild. Dealer's choice of five-card stud or draw."

"That sounds fair enough to me," Longarm said. "And I've held up your game long enough." He pulled one of the chairs from the wall up to the table, Ross moving his chair to make room. As Pete moved to take the vacant chair at Longarm's left, Longarm glanced at the stacks of silver dollars and took four double-eagles from his pocket. As he laid them on the table he said, "I guess I'll have to buy some playing money from whoever can spare it."

"Be glad to oblige you, Custis," Pete said. "You want all four of them changed?"

"Oh, I'll just cripple along with half of it to start out," Longarm replied casually. "I feel like I'm due for a streak, so after the first hand or two I'll be playing outa my winnings."

"Well, now, let's just see about that," Bates said as Pete began stacking silver dollars in front of Longarm. He tossed a cartwheel into the center of the table. "First ante's in, men, so pony up. Pete, get busy and deal them cards."

"We'll make it stud this round," Pete announced, shuffling with the skill of a professional.

Silver dollars thunked into the center of the table while Pete shuffled a second time and put the cards in front of Longarm to cut. While Longarm cut the deck, Pete raked the house cut from the money on the table before picking up the cards. With quick, skillful flicks of his pudgy fingers he dropped cards face down around the table in front of Sam, Bates, Brown, Ross, and Longarm in turn, gave himself one, and while the other players looked at their hole cards dealt each man a second card face up.

His face expressionless, Longarm watched the pasteboards fall on the blanket. The deuce of spades lay in front of Sam, Bates had gotten the jack of diamonds, Brown the eight of clubs, Ross the ten of hearts, the diamond ten lay in front of him, and Poker Pete had dealt himself the eight of hearts.

"Jack bets," Pete announced.

Bates tossed a cartwheel into the pot and the others followed his action. Pete flipped a new round of cards: the trey of diamonds to Sam, the six of clubs to Bates, the diamond ace to Brown, the hearts nine to Ross, the seven of spades to Longarm, and the four of hearts in front of himself.

"Going to bet your ace, Shuteye?" Pete asked.

"I guess," Brown replied, tossing out a dollar. "Even if I ain't got anything to go with it."

With two cards still to come, and no sign of a good hand showing among the cards turned face up on the table, the other players met Brown's bet. Pete dealt the next cards. Sam got the diamond five, Bates the six of spades, the ace of clubs fell to Brown, the four of hearts to Ross, Longarm received the ten of spades, and Pete dealt himself the eight of spades.

"You can't complain any longer, Brown," the dealer commented. "Sitting there with aces up. You're on top of everybody else right now, but we're all pushing you."

"I figure these aces are worth a couple of dollars apiece," Brown said as he stacked up four cartwheels and shoved them into the pot. "You men game to go along?"

One by one, the other players met the bet. Longarm, with a ten in the hole to match the pair turned face up on the table, could see that barring the possibility of Brown's hole card being an ace, he had the game's best hand. His face expressionless, he waited for Pete to deal the fourth cards.

On the final round, Sam got a six, Bates a second jack, Brown another eight, Ross the queen of hearts, Longarm another seven, and Pete the nine of diamonds.

Ross shook his head, stacked his cards, and said, "That's all for me."

"Just look at that, will you," Pete chuckled, nodding at Brown's cards. "I ain't wishing you no bad luck, Shuteye, but if it was me, I'd just as soon not be sitting on that start of the dead man's hand you got."

"I'm not Wild Bill Hickock," Brown said without any inflection in his voice as he pushed a stack of ten silver dollars into the pot. "But my ace-high pairs look pretty good, so I'll bet 'em for ten."

Ross laid his hole card face down, swept up the four hearts

that lay in front of him, and dropped them on the hole card. "A man's a fool to bluff when he's beat with what's showing," he remarked.

Longarm said nothing, but pushed ten dollars into the pot.

"Well, now," Poker Pete said thoughtfully. "Custis, if you ain't bluffing, you got a full house. Question one is if you got it, question two is whether it's high to the sevens or the tens. But I ain't fool enough to buck you. I'll fold."

"Looking at what's on the table, I'd be a fool to stay," Sam announced, gathering his cards up.

"It's up to you, Bates," Pete said. "Raise or show."

"Oh, I'm raising," Bates replied. "Twenty, this time."

"And twenty more," Longarm said, adding his bet to the heap of coins in the table's center.

"Well, I'll have to see you."

"I'm just stubborn enough to stay in, even if you've got that third ten," Ross agreed, adding another twenty dollars to the pot. "And I don't think you've got it. I'll call."

Longarm flipped over the third ten. Ross shrugged and gathered up his hand. Pete shoved the pot to Longarm.

"Well, Custis, you got off to a good start," he said. "Now let's see if you can hold on to it."

For the next hour the game went on, luck seesawing between the five players, none of them winning or losing consistently. Then Longarm noticed a subtle change in the flow of winnings as Bates began raking in more and more of the big pots. Longarm's stacks of silver dollars dwindled, as did those of all the gamblers except Bates. He began watching both Bates and Poker Pete more closely, and after twenty minutes and half a dozen hands went by he finally saw what he'd been looking for.

Betting a pat hand in a round of draw, Ross had laid down a straight flush from the nine with the joker substituting for the king. The hand had been long in playing, and the bets had been substantial. Longarm had not relaxed his vigilance, but if he had not been concentrating on the dealer's movements he would almost certainly have missed the quick flicker of Pete's pudgy fingers as he palmed the joker when gathering the cards and then substituted it for the first card he dealt to Bates.

Longarm said nothing, but let the game go on. He stayed in the pot despite a mediocre hand as Bates and Poker Pete whipsawed the betting higher and higher. When the other players began to show increasing reluctance to stay in the pot and the pile of money in center of the table had grown so high that none of them had enough cash remaining in front of them to continue, he slid his Colt out quietly, his movement hidden by the table.

As Longarm had anticipated, Pete finally called. Longarm lifted his Colt and thudded its butt down on the table.

His voice cold, he announced, "The game's over."

Bates made a gesture to draw, but Longarm swivelled the muzzle of his revolver to cover him.

"What in hell you doing, Custis?" Poker Pete demanded.

"You heard me, Pete," Longarm replied, his tone icy. "I just called the game off. You and your partner's been cheating us for the last hour or more."

"Now, wait a minute!" Bates began.

Longarm broke in, "I didn't mention your name, Bates, so I reckon you just gave the show away."

Ross shook his head, frowning, then said, "Maybe you'd better explain, Custis."

"How many pots have you raked in this past hour?" he asked, not taking his eyes off Pete and Bates.

"Why—two, maybe three little ones," Ross replied. His eyes widened and he went on, "Come to think of it, Pete and Bates *have* been the big winners."

"So they have," Brown agreed. "Look at the money in front of them!"

"Maybe you better tell us how they worked it, Custis," Sam suggested.

"Turn up that hand Bates was betting," Longarm said. When Sam reached over and flipped Bates's cards face up, he revealed three aces and the joker. Longarm went on, "I seen Pete palm that joker when he gathered the cards last time. Now, I ain't been counting, but it seems to me either him or Bates has held that kicker an awful lot this past hour."

"By God, they have!" Ross agreed. "I'll bet Pete's been palming it all along!"

"What're we going to do about it?" Brown asked. "Damn it, I've been sitting in this game out here almost every night for the past week, and I've gone away loser all but one night! These bastards owe me a lot of money!"

"There's not any law we can go to," Sam said. "We're not in Deming out here, so the town marshal can't do anything."

"That's right," Longarm agreed. "About all you can do is take what money you come here with outa that pot, and call it quits."

"Well, I don't know about you other men," Ross put in, "but I'd settle for that."

"I guess I would, too," they agreed.

"Go ahead and take out what you brought here with you," Longarm said. "That's what I aim to do. I'll leave it to you to get back what's yours. You know how much you're out."

As the others began taking money from the table and pocketing it, Poker Pete asked Longarm, "What in hell brought you out here in the first place, Custis? You some kind of lawman?"

Instead of trying to spin a yarn to cover his real interest, Longarm ignored Pete's question and replied with one of his own. He asked, "Now, if I was, don't you think I'd've just arrested you and your partner?"

"I don't know what for," Bates said quickly. "New Mexico Territory hasn't got a law against gambling, even if some of the towns like Deming do."

"I'll settle my business with you in private," Longarm said, "after these other men are gone."

How're we going to get back to town?" Brown asked. "I hate to start walking them eight or nine miles at this time of night."

"We'll just take Pete's surrey," Ross replied. "Let him and his partner hoof it to their next stop."

"I'd rather you didn't do that," Longarm said quickly. "I been sorta figuring on using it myself, after I finish the business I got with these two."

"Don't worry," Sam said. I've got my wagon outside. I was going on home when I got out of the game, but it won't be any trouble to take you men into Deming."

"Just where do you fit into this, Custis?" Brown asked. "I

87

heard what you told Poker Pete a minute ago. You didn't give him a straight answer, and now my curiosity's stirred up."

"All I can tell you is I got my own reasons," Longarm said. "And you ain't going to get no more outa me if you stand there asking questions all night."

Brown nodded. "I don't suppose we've got any right to poke into your private affairs," he said. "I'm just glad you came along when you did. You've saved me and the others a lot of money tonight. Whatever your business is, good luck!"

"I feel like Brown does," Sam said. "Thanks." He turned to the others and went on, "Now, if you men are ready, let's get back to town and leave Custis to finish up his business."

When the hoofbeats of Sam's wagon team had died away, Poker Pete asked Longarm, "Who in hell are you, anyhow? I'll bet a dollar to a pile of horse shit that whatever your name is, it sure ain't Custis!"

"Now, maybe you'd win that bet and maybe you'd lose it," Longarm replied. "But my name ain't got a thing to do with what I want outa you two."

"Just exactly what is that?" Bates asked. "It sure as hell isn't money, or you'd've taken what those other fellows lost as well as what's left on the table."

"Oh, it ain't money," Longarm replied. "I figure you two men have got the answers to some questions I'm going to ask you."

"What kind of questions?" Poker Pete demanded.

"You'll find out soon enough," Longarm told him. "Before I start asking, I'll just take your guns and pick up what money I got coming back. Then we'll get down to business, and if you two want to walk outa here instead of being carried out feet first, you better tell me what I want to know!"

Chapter 10

Under the menacing muzzle of Longarm's Colt, the two gamblers surrendered their weapons. Poker Pete put a .31 Remington-Smoot on the table and Bates deposited a .38 tip-up Smith & Wesson.

Longarm felt better when he saw the guns they carried. No outlaw who lived in the shadow of constant danger would have risked using such weapons. He was sure now that Poker Pete and Bates were gamblers and drifters rather than outlaws, men who moved on the fringe of lawlessness, not outright criminals, but who had contacts with the criminal element. He pulled their guns to his side of the table where Pete and Bates could not reach them easily and holstered his Colt.

"Now," he told them, "maybe you'll give me some answers."

"I don't know what kind of questions you'd ask that we can answer," Bates said. "But ask away."

"I don't have to tell you that I just blew into town," Longarm began. "And I need some information real fast."

"What kind of information?" Pete asked.

"Well, I don't fancy staying at that hotel downtown. I hear the Deming marshal's tougher'n a boot sole," Longarm replied.

Bates's eyes narrowed. He said, "What you mean is, you're looking for a hideout. Am I right?"

"About halfway between right and wrong," Longarm said. "I'd like to know about a place where I ain't apt to be noticed."

"You didn't come out here just to sit in on a poker game, then, did you?" Pete asked.

"Not exactly. I've found out that men in your business pretty generally know their way around, and being a stranger here I got to find out who'd be a good connection for me, somebody who'd have a place to stay where I don't have to worry about watching my back every minute."

"You're saying you're on the dodge?" Pete scowled.

"A man in my trade moves around a lot," Longarm replied, sticking to the exact truth. "I don't need to tell you that." Then, still being equally truthful, he added quickly, "But if there's any Wanteds out on me, I ain't heard about 'em."

"Suppose you tell us what kind of information you're after," Bates suggested.

"There's a whisper moving on the grapevine that the Santa Fe railroad's lost some right valuable property outa their depot here," Longarm answered. "If it's as important as I've heard, they oughta pay a real good-sized amount to get it back."

"Where'd you pick that up?" Pete frowned. "We haven't heard about it."

"Well, they sure wouldn't be yelling the word from the church steeple, now would they?" Longarm demanded. "Never mind where I heard about it. That's my affair."

"What is it they've lost? A shipment of some kind?" Bates asked.

"That's my affair, too," Longarm said curtly.

"Maybe you won't mind telling us where you heard about whatever it is?" Pete suggested.

"On the way to Santa Fe I passed through them mountains south of Trinidad," Longarm replied, still sticking to the exact truth and letting Pete and Bates draw their own conclusions and inferences. "If you've ever been there, you'll know there's damned little happening that the men hiding out in 'em miss."

Bates nodded slowly. "I know what you mean, Custis." He turned to Pete. "I guess he's all right. He knows the right places, anyhow."

"Funny we've never heard his name before," Pete said.

"By now you ought to've figured out that Custis ain't the name I always travel under," Longarm said casually. He was feeling on more solid ground now that the two seemed ready to accept his yarn. "You might've heard about me by another one, but that's neither here nor there."

"What's this information you're after worth to you, Custis?" Bates asked. "If it's real important, I guess we ought to be sorta partners."

"I don't work with partners," Longarm said coldly. "And it might be I'm here on a bad tip. It might be that even if I dig up that . . . well, whatever's missing . . . and sell it back to the Santa Fe, they wouldn't be real big-hearted."

"Just the same, fair's fair," Pete said quickly. "If we give you a hand and you cash in, we oughta get a share."

Longarm remained silent for a moment. Then he nodded slowly and said, "I'll grant you that's how the game's played. I can't argue that. I'd feel the same way, was I you."

"What's it worth, then?" Bates demanded.

"It'd have to be a percent," Longarm replied. "Because this ain't like it is when there's a reward posted. I ain't sure yet the railroad's going to make a payout. And if I don't make anything, there won't be no pot to split."

"That's reasonable," Poker Pete nodded. "Me and Bates would understand that."

"Five percent, then," Longarm told them.

"Fifteen," Bates countered.

"That means you'll settle for ten," Longarm shot back.

"Ten's fair," Pete agreed.

Bates nodded his agreement and then said, "We still don't know what you're after, Custis."

"What I'm after is a shipment that was sent here two, maybe three weeks ago, from the Santa Fe main office in Chicago. From what I been told, it just dropped outa sight and nobody knows where it is except whoever's got it now."

"It's a hell of a long way from here to Chicago," Bates said thoughtfully. "Are you sure it ever got here?"

"From what I been told, it did," Longarm said.

"And nobody knows what's in it?" Pete frowned.

"I guess whoever sent it from Chicago knows," Longarm told him. "But that don't help to find out."

"Has the Santa Fe put up a reward?" Pete asked.

"Not yet. They're still trying to act like it ain't been lost," Longarm said. "Now, the way I figure it, somebody here found out that shipment was on the way, and grabbed it off before anybody knew it had got here."

Bates and Poker Pete exchanged glances. Then Pete turned to Longarm and said, "The man you better go see is Sam

Carson. I guess you've heard his name? Maybe even know him?"

"I've heard his name," Longarm nodded, not bothering to add that he'd also seen it on Wanted flyers several years before. "He cut a pretty wide swatch for a while, then he just sorta dropped outa sight. I never did hear what happened to him, just figured he was dead by now."

"Sam got shot up pretty bad," Bates said. "He was the boss of Hell on Wheels when the Santa Fe was pushing tracks to Deming. He holed up out on the prairie and couldn't do much until just a little while back. Then he began stirring again."

"And he's still around?" Longarm asked.

"He sure as hell is," Pete replied. "Got him a place out from town about ten miles. But he never did get outa touch with his boys from the Hell-on-Wheels days. Even when he was just getting better, he kept them going. They didn't do much close to Deming, but they been keeping busy back up the line toward Albuquerque, and down toward El Paso."

"I guess he's got the town marshal in his pocket, too?" Longarm suggested.

"Not so's you'd notice," Bates replied. "That Buck Tyler's an independent son of a bitch. Far as I know, he ain't one of Sam's boys. If he was, we'd be running this game in the middle of town instead of out here in the sticks."

"This place of Sam's . . . you suppose it'd be a good place for a man on the dodge to stay a while?" Longarm asked.

"You said you wasn't running," Bates frowned.

"I ain't. But, like I told you, I feel sorta uneasy at that hotel. And I'll need a hole to jump into if I pull off this little stunt," Longarm answered. "If a man was to find that package the Santa Fe's after, he'd want a safe place to stay while he dickered with 'em over it."

"That makes sense," Pete agreed. "And I can't think of a better place than Sam's got. It's a mite far out of town, but you won't likely be bothered there."

"How do I go about finding it?"

"Just take the west fork of the road you came out here on instead of bearing north," Pete told him. "You can't miss Sam's place; it's an old adobe set on a little rise about a mile off of the trail."

"I'll be heading out there tomorrow, then," Longarm said. "And I hate to make you men wait, but I'm going to have to leave you here a while. I'll need your rig to get back to town in. But I'll send the liveryman out to get you, and I'll give him your guns to bring back."

"Now, hold on!" Bates protested. "We're supposed to be in cahoots on this!"

"Cahoots or not, I don't aim to risk my skin when I don't have to," Longarm said flatly. "Now, I'm sorry to put you out, but that's the way it's going to be!"

Scooping up the gamblers' guns from the table, Longarm backed out the door. He stood for a few minutes in the darkness, watching the door while he let his eyes adjust to night vision. When neither Poker Pete nor Bates came out, he walked around the soddie and found the surrey, its horse hitched and ready. A short time later, after delivering the surrey to the liveryman and telling him to return it, he was back in his hotel room.

It ain't been a bad night, old son, Longarm silently told his mirrored image as he stood in front of the bureau uncorking the bottle of Tom Moore. He tilted the bottle to his lips. *Now all you got to do is find Sam Carson and see if you can pull a little wool down over his eyes, too. Carson's a lot smarter'n them two tinhorns, and he ain't going to be all that easy to fool, but if there's anybody in spitting distance of this place who'd know about a crook stealing that suitcase, he'd sure be the man.*

Lighting a final cheroot, Longarm finished undressing and went through his usual pre-bedtime routine of arranging his clothing where it would be easily reached in the morning. He placed his Colt in a chair beside the bed, within easy reach of his hand. His day had been longer than usual, and though the mattress was lumpy, the sheets unironed, and the pillow limp, he was asleep within a few moments.

But even weariness and deep sleep did not blunt Longarm's keen senses. As always when in strange surroundings, he slept with one ear open. The almost noiseless scratching at his door brought him fully awake and the Colt was in his hand by the time his reaction to the sound brought him upright in bed. The tiny rasping on the door panel sounded again. Rolling out of the bed, Longarm crossed the room, moving noiselessly on his bare feet.

Raising his voice only enough to be sure it would be heard through the door panel, he asked, "Who're you looking for?"

A woman's voice answered. Like his own, it was only loud enough to pass through the wooden door. "Marshal Long? Let me in, please! It's Anita."

Recognizing the voice as that of Anita Bradley, he replied, "Just a minute. I got to put some clothes on first."

Grabbing his trousers, Longarm slid into them and padded on bare feet back to the door. He unlocked it and opened it wide enough to allow the Pinkerton operative to slip from the dimly lighted hallway into his room.

Anita's head was covered by a hood, and the long cloak she had on concealed all but a few inches of her long white Harvey House waitress uniform. She stood away from the door while Longarm closed and locked it. He took a match from the pocket of the vest he'd hung on the chair by the bed and lighted the lamp that stood on the bureau. The bottle of Tom Moore glinting in the lamplight caught his eye.

"I don't reckon it'd bother you if I have a swallow of this before we start talking," he said, picking up the bottle. "And if you'd care for one . . ."

"Why, thank you, Marshal. I could use a drink after the kind of day this has been, and you know how much chance I have of getting one at the Harvey House."

"I thought we wasn't going to be so all-fired polite and hoity-toity," Longarm said as he moved to the wash-stand, where two glasses stood beside the water pitcher and washbowl.

"We did, didn't we?" Anita smiled. She went on, "Don't bother with water for me, Longarm. I like good whiskey as much as a man does."

Longarm poured a generous tot of the rye into the glass and handed it to Anita, then said, "I'll sip right outa the bottle, if you don't mind." He started toward the bed, saw Anita standing with the glass in her hand, and went on, "I'll get you a chair, too, Nita. Since what you got to tell me was important enough to bring you here in the shank of the night, I imagine it's going to take a little time to tell it."

Going to the wall where the room's other chair stood, he moved it to the foot of the bed. Anita sat down and waited while Longarm settled down on the side of the bed, fished a long slim cigar from his vest pocket, and lighted it. As he puffed the cigar into a glow he glanced at Anita and found her eyes fixed on him. He raised the bottle of Moore and said, "Now we're comfortable, we'll wet our whistles and then start talking."

After she'd sipped the whiskey, Anita said somewhat hesitantly, "I hope you don't mind me disturbing you, Longarm, but I thought it'd be easier for us to talk here than while you're eating breakfast at the Harvey House."

"If you got something we need to talk about, I don't mind one bit," Longarm assured her. "If you figured it was important enough to come into town for, I'd say you done the right thing."

"I didn't even know whether you'd checked in to the hotel yet," she went on. "The desk clerk was sound asleep when I got into the lobby, but the register was on the desk, so I looked up your room number and came upstairs without having to wake him."

"It's a good thing you didn't get here till now. I just got in few minutes ago."

"You've been out running down leads?"

"There ain't all that many leads to run down," Longarm reminded her. "I figured I'd have to make my own."

"And did you?"

"More or less. I got a place to start looking after sunup."

"Then I suppose I did right in coming to talk to you," she nodded. "What I heard when I was talking with the girls after supper might help you."

"Anything's going to help right now, Nita," Longarm said. "I ain't got too much to go on."

"Your leads don't look promising, then?"

"It's too soon to know," he told her. "What I found out is that an old outlaw named Sam Carson has been holed up for quite a while just outside of town. Seems he got shot up pretty bad in a gunfight a few months back and needed a quiet place to go till he got healed up."

"Do you think he's the one who stole the suitcase?"

"I ain't making a judgement till I do some more digging. Like I said, all I know about Carson is his reputation, but if there's any crooked work going on in a hundred miles of where he's at, he'd be one that'd likely know about it."

"Do you think you can get him to talk to you?"

"I figure to get him to open up, one way or another."

Anita nodded slowly, "Yes, I think you will. I have an idea that when you start out to do something, you won't be satisfied or stop until you've done it."

"I take that as a compliment, Nita, so I thank you. But what's got you stirred up enough to bring you here at this time of the night?"

"I'm afraid my information's almost as sketchy as yours," she said. She drained the remaining whiskey from her glass. "That really tastes good, Longarm."

"Think you could use a refill?"

"I . . . yes, I can. It's been a long day and we've got some more talking to do."

She held out her glass and Longarm stood up, stepped to her chair, and poured another inch or so of rye into it. When he sat down after returning to the bed, he was again aware that her eyes had been following his movements.

Nita took a quick sip of the whiskey and went on, "After we'd cleared the tables after supper and all of us were up in our room talking while we got ready for bed, one of the girls said something about what she'd overheard when she served supper to Buck Tyler and his deputy."

"Peters," Longarm nodded. "I run into him when I stopped in to tell Tyler that Carstow'd been shot. What'd they say?"

"It didn't make much sense, but it bothered me."

"Was Tyler and Peters talking about them missing bonds?"

"No. At least, if they were, it didn't mean anything to Janet. That's the girl who was waiting on their table. I don't suppose you understand about waiting on tables, do you?"

"Well, I never worked at waiting on folks, but I eat at

restaurants all the time." Longarm was again aware that Nita was watching him. "What're you getting at, Nita?"

"For one thing, the people you're serving don't pay much attention to you unless you're putting their plates down or taking them away. If you come up to refill a glass or a coffee cup, usually they just go on talking."

"I guess you hear a few interesting things, don't you?"

"Once in a while you'll hear things you aren't intended to," she smiled. "Now, another thing you need to understand is that you're back and forth a lot, so you'll hear little bits and pieces of what the customers are saying. Most of the time you don't pay much attention to their talk, because you don't hear enough for it to mean anything."

"I can see that," he nodded. "And you've given me an idea, Nita. I'd imagine you and the other girls hear a lot of things that I might like to know about. I'm going to talk to the manager of that Harvey House and see can I get him to let me put the whole bunch of 'em to work, listening and passing on what they hear."

"Stool pigeons?" Nita frowned. "They'd be amateurs."

"Sure. But it's little bits and pieces like what you been telling me that helps make a case sometimes."

"Well, it might work," she agreed. "It certainly won't hurt to try. And it'd give me an excuse to talk to you when I feel like I need to."

"I'll think about it some more," Longarm told her. "But go on with what you was telling me about what Tyler and Peters was saying."

"They were talking about burying something to keep the coyotes from getting to it. Could it have been the suitcase?"

"Well, I never seen a coyote yet that'd turn up his nose at much of anything he could get his teeth into," Longarm frowned. "If that suitcase was a leather one, and a pack of 'em run onto it laying loose out on the desert, they'd sure eat it."

"I don't suppose there'd be much chance of us finding it before the coyotes got to it, would there?"

"Not much. There's a lot of desert out from town," Longarm said, thinking aloud. "If somebody was to bury something out in it, I'd say they'd be the only one that might ever have a chance of finding it again. They didn't say anything about landmarks, I guess?"

"If they did, Janet didn't hear it. What caught her attention later was when one of them mentioned bones."

"Burying bones?"

Nita shook her head. "I don't know. She was away from the table when they changed the subject. But I just mentioned what she heard about bones because it struck me as being a funny thing for them to be talking about. What I started to tell you when I remembered their talking about bones was that something else Janet heard seems to me to tie the Santa Fe into what they were saying."

"What was that?"

"Well, she didn't remember whether it was the marshal or the deputy who was talking, but one of them made a remark about a bunkhouse car. Doesn't that mean the same thing to you that it did to me? A railroad car on the Santa Fe?"

"It sure does," Longarm agreed. "It'd have to be one of them old boxcars the railroad fixed up with bunks and such for their track workers to sleep in."

"There are a dozen or so cars like that on sidings in the Santa Fe yards right now," Nita said. "I saw them when I came in the other day."

"So there are," he nodded. "I didn't pay much attention to the cars. I been too busy. But I'll sure go through 'em with a fine-tooth comb when it's daylight."

"That will be all too soon," Nita said, standing up. Longarm stood also. She went on, "And I've got to get back to the Harvey House." She took a step toward the door, turned suddenly, and looked him squarely in the face. "But I don't think I want to go back. Would you mind if I spent the rest of the night with you, Longarm?"

Chapter 11

Though Longarm was totally unprepared for Nita's question, he did not let his surprise show on his face. He said, "Why, I'd be right pleased if you stayed, Nita. I'd imagine any man you asked that question would be."

"I thought you'd answer just about that way," Nita smiled.

Longarm said, "I'd be a plain fool not to. You're a right pretty woman, Nita. I take your invitation as a compliment."

Nita took a Baby Le Mat revolver out of a hidden sheath inside her cloak and laid it on the chair in which she'd been sitting. Then she shrugged out of the hooded cloak and dropped it on the chair over the pistol. Her fingers moved to the line of black buttons that ran from the high neck of her dress to the waist and she began undoing them.

"I'm sure I'm not the first woman who's found you attractive enough to invite you to bed with her," she told Longarm.

"Maybe so and maybe not," he answered. "It ain't my way to talk about womenfolks a lot."

"Men who appeal to women seldom do; I'll give them credit for that. And I don't make a habit of inviting every man I meet to hop into bed with me."

"Now, it never entered my mind that you did, Nita," Long-arm protested.

Nita had reached the last button of her dress by now and was shrugging it off her shoulders. She watched Longarm as she stepped out of the dress and draped it over the chair with the cape. She smiled as his eyes travelled over her body, taking in the full breasts that bulged under a thin voile camisole and the dark vee that was visible above her thighs through the sheer fabric of her knee-length pantalets.

"This time, I saw that you weren't going to be the first to ask," she went on. "So I decided it was up to me."

"Well, we're both in about the same boat, I'd say," he replied. "We move around all the time and don't stay in one place long enough to do much courting."

"I had my fill of formal courting when I was younger," Nita confessed. "Not that it should matter a great deal, but I've been married twice. If a woman's still bashful after her first marriage, the second one's guaranteed to cure her, especially if she's widowed twice."

"Both of your husbands died?"

She nodded. "My first was a cavalry officer who got killed in the Indian wars, and my second was another Pinkerton operative who was shot three years ago when he tried to arrest a stock swindler he'd caught up with."

"I'm sorry to hear that, Nita," Longarm said. "Sounds to me like you've had a pretty tough time."

"I'm not crying about my life, Longarm. Given enough time, you can get over just about anything."

"This line of work we're in ain't exactly like singing in a church choir," Longarm observed. "You want me to blow out the lamp, or leave it on?"

"Suit yourself," she replied. Then she added quickly, "No, go on and blow it out. We've reached the point where I think I'd enjoy feeling you more than just looking at you."

"There ain't any rule I know about that says you can't do both," he observed.

"No. But when they're in the dark, people will sometimes let themselves go a lot more freely than they will if the room's lighted."

"You got a point there, Nita," Longarm agreed. "I'll blow out the lamp, then."

Longarm stepped to the dresser. He glanced at Nita and saw that she'd taken off her chemise and was stepping out of her underpants. His last glimpse before he blew out the lamp and plunged the room into darkness was of her high firm breasts with their large ruddy-pink rosettes, hips swelling below a small waist, and a scanty dark pubic brush at the apex of firm sculptured thighs.

He started for the bed, unbuckling his belt as he moved, and sensed rather than saw Nita a moment before their bodies brushed together in the gloom. Letting his trousers slide to the floor, Longarm quickly brought up his hands and grasped her an instant before they collided in the darkness.

Nita placed a hand on his forearm to steady herself, and for a moment they stood motionless in the darkness. Then Nita took a short quick step to bring them together. Longarm felt her soft, swelling breasts pressing against the coarse curls that covered his muscular chest.

She began twisting her shoulders from side to side, rubbing the protruding tips of her breast against the coarse curls on Longarm's chest. The faint aroma of the light perfume she wore rose from her warm body, and he was aware of the softness of her skin where it touched him. Then he felt a small shudder ripple through her and she pulled herself away.

"We really haven't had enough time to get acquainted," she whispered. "Let's stand here for a minute before we go to bed."

Longarm turned toward her, freeing his feet from the huddle of his trousers. Nita's free hand brushed over his shoulder and down his side to his hips, her fingers pausing for a moment each time they encountered one of the scars left from old encounters with the lawless. Then her hand reached his hips and slid over to close around his burgeoning erection.

"I've been wanting to hold you this way since I saw those muscles in your arms and shoulders," she told him. "I was sure a man built like you are above the waist must have a lot down here to give a woman."

Longarm did not reply. His head was bent to Nita's generous breasts, his lips and tongue moving gently over their cushioned swells as he sought her rosettes. He moved from one protruding tip to the other, caressing the pebbled rosettes with quick flicks of his tongue and rubbing his cheeks over them. Nita's hands were busy at his groin, fondling his swelling shaft, squeezing him gently as he grew firm in response to the caresses of her soft fingers.

After a few minutes she whispered hoarsely, "I don't want to wait any longer. Take me to bed, Longarm."

Picking her up, Longarm carried Nita the few steps to the bed and lowered her to the mattress. As he knelt beside her, Nita's hand closed around his rigid shaft and tugged him gently.

"Come up here where I can reach you," she said softly.

Longarm straddled Nita's body, kneeling above her. For a few moments she held his swollen heft between her fingers. Then she leaned forward and rubbed its sensitive tip over her soft cheeks before closing her lips over the tip and engulfing him.

For several moments Nita remained motionless, her head pressed against Longarm's groin. Then she drew back and he felt her tongue rasping gently over his tip, while a soft susurrus of delight, like the purr of a contented cat, rose from her throat. She held him engulfed a short while longer, keeping up the caresses of her agile tongue. Then he felt her body begin to quiver and she drew her head back, releasing him.

"Hurry, Longarm!" she gasped. "I'm burning up to have you in me now!"

Longarm wasted no time. He slid down Nita's trembling body and she spread her thighs to let him kneel between them. She grasped his engorged shaft, guiding him, and Longarm plunged into her. He drove full length with a swift, hard thrust and held himself buried for a moment, Nita's hips writhing and pushing up against his. Then he began to stroke with piston-like lunges while Nita cried out with delight, her body trembling in response to the rhythmic rising and falling of his hips.

"Now, Longarm, now!" she cried after a moment.

Nita's body arched as Longarm increased the tempo of his stroking, and her trembling soon became a wild, abandoned tossing as she writhed under him. She rolled her hips from side to side and her cries rose to a crescendo of quick small shrieks. Then she stiffened for an instant before she began quivering uncontrollably.

Longarm stopped stroking then and held himself buried full-length, pressing firmly against her until Nita's shrieks died away to a low contented murmuring which ended in a series of small gusty sighs. After a while the sighs trickled off to silence. Her tossing and quivering faded and she lay still and limp beneath him.

Longarm did not release the pressure of his hips against her and after a few moments had ticked away, Nita stirred and said,

"I knew I was right about you, Longarm. You're the man I've been needing for a long time. I couldn't wait to go off with you this time, and I can tell from what I feel that you're ready to give me a lot more, so start again whenever you're ready."

"If you're ready, I am too," Longarm told her.

He began to stroke again, slowly and deliberately, almost gently, while Nita lay supine. When her response began he speeded the tempo of his thrusting, and this time he did not hold back when Nita's hips started rising to meet his lunges. He drove deeper and faster until her cries of delight rose in the darkness and her body began jerking uncontrollably.

Even when Nita's spasm peaked, Longarm held back again. He waited until her frantic movements slackened and faded, then resumed his long deep driving. Each time he completed one of his penetrating lunges, he stopped and held himself pressed to her while she twisted her hips to get the greatest pleasure possible from the pressure of his impaling shaft.

This time, Nita did not respond as quickly as she had earlier. Long minutes passed before her body grew taut and her breathing ragged. Longarm lowered his head and sought her lips as he kept up his steady, driving pace. She thrust her tongue into his mouth and he met it with his and held their kiss until Nita's head began rolling uncontrollably on the pillow. Her hips went once again into the frantic jerking and tossing that had preceded her earlier orgasms.

He drove faster then, and arched his back to plunge into her still deeper. Soon Nita's small, frantic cries of mounting ecstasy broke the night. When he felt her trembling into the final throes that marked the peak of her spasm he relaxed his own control and jetted. He pressed hard against her while her hips heaved and twisted and her cries mounted to a final, sharp scream.

Then he allowed himself to relax and they lay trembling, still joined by their fleshy bond until their shaking ended. Nita sighed, a long exhalation, that ended only when she'd grown completely limp and Longarm lay quietly on her softly quivering body.

Minutes passed while they lay without speaking. Then Nita

103

stirred and said, "I'd like to have an encore right now, Longarm, but it's getting awfully late, and we've both got jobs to think about."

"I ain't forgetting that," he replied. "I know you got to get back to the Harvey House in time for breakfast."

Longarm lifted himself off the bed and reached into the pocket of his vest that hung on the chair beside it. He took out a cigar and match, scraped his steel-hard thumbnail over the match-head, and lighted the cigar. He looked at Nita over the flickering flame of the match. She was stretched out in total relaxation, her generous body sprawled on the tousled bed, a contented smile on her face.

"I'll get there in plenty of time," she said. "But you'd better light the lamp before that match burns out."

Longarm stepped over to the bureau and managed to touch the match to the lamp wick before its flame touched his fingertips.

Nita had risen and was moving toward the chair on which her clothes hung when Longarm turned around. Her face was serious now, and she began dressing in a businesslike manner.

As she pulled on her camisole she remarked, "I thought Allan Pinkerton was strict until I ran into Fred Harvey's rules. Mr. Harvey believes in keeping his girls on a very short tether."

"Well, I sure wouldn't want you to lose your job on my account, and get in trouble with Pinkerton's head office."

"Oh, I won't be in any trouble," Nita assured Longarm as she pulled her dress over her head and started smoothing into place. "I don't know about the other Harvey Houses, but the girls here manage to slip away just about any night they want to. Even if I'm a few minutes late, they'll cover up for me."

"It's still real dark," Longarm said, lifting a corner of the window shade to peer out. "Maybe I better get dressed and walk back with you."

"Don't even think of it," she replied. "I'm a big girl, Longarm. I've got my pistol, and I'm not afraid to use it if I have to. Besides, it isn't very far to the Harvey House."

"I'll be moving into that office coach in the Santa Fe yards that Carstow used," Longarm told her as he picked up the bottle of Tom Moore and tilted it. "It's a lot closer to the Harvey

House than this hotel. You can get to it in about two minutes any time you feel inclined to pay me a visit."

"That'll be tonight and every night as long as we're both here," she replied quickly. "You know, I feel like a schoolgirl again, Longarm. There's nothing like being in bed with a good man to make a woman feel young again."

"I feel right good myself," he replied. He offered her the bottle, but she shook her head.

"No," she said. "I don't want to report for work with liquor on my breath. I've worked so hard to keep my cover job that I wouldn't do anything that might mean losing it."

"Can't say I blame you," he agreed as she moved toward the door. "You go ahead, then. I'll be over after a while to get some breakfast. I want to get started early; there's a lot of leads I need to follow up on today."

Longarm reached the Harvey House before the breakfast rush began. Only a few of the tables were occupied and the waitresses were standing around the kitchen door, chatting in whispers while waiting for new arrivals. George Forbes was sitting at one of the tables. He saw Longarm come in and motioned for him to join him.

"I was expecting you to come out last night and tell me what happened when you talked to Buck Tyler," he said as Longarm settled into the chair across from him. "But I suppose something detained you until it was too late."

"I got a mite tied up," Longarm nodded. "I was figuring I'd stop by after breakfast and see you. I'm right sorry I didn't make it last night. Hope I didn't put you out none."

"Don't worry about it, Marshal," Forbes replied. "I can understand how it must be when you're on a case."

"I wouldn't've had much to tell you even if I'd got there," Longarm went on. "I been wondering how you got along with Buck Tyler, though. He didn't give you no trouble, did he?"

"Not a bit. If anything, he was a little bit more cooperative than usual."

"He took care of everything, I guess?"

"Yes, indeed. And I told the maintenance crew to clean up Carstow's car and get it ready for you. You can move in this afternoon, whenever you find time."

"Well, thanks, Mr. Forbes. I'll sure do just that." Longarm nodded as Nita came up to take his order. Her manner gave no hint that she and Longarm had ever met before. He ordered his usual fried eggs, potatoes, and ham, and after Nita had left he picked up his conversation with the Santa Fe man. "There's one or two things I need to find out from you."

"Go ahead."

"Tyler and his deputy was talking about a bunkhouse car. I ain't got the beginning of an idea what it's got to do with anything. It might not mean much, but I ain't got all that many leads on this case, so I figure I better try to find out."

Frowning thoughtfully, Forbes said, "We've got a number of bunkhouse cars on sidings in the yards, waiting for the time when we'll be pushing iron again. I suppose Tyler and Peters could have been talking about them."

"It's been a while since I was in one of them cars," Longarm said. "As I recall, they're just boxcars with a lot of bunks built up inside 'em."

"That's right," Forbes said. "Three tiers of bunks on each side. A car will sleep about forty men."

"They'd sure be packed in, wouldn't they?"

"Pretty tightly," Forbes agreed. "A bunkhouse car doesn't provide the kind of accommodations you'd expect at a hotel."

"With all them little bunks in it, a car like that sure would be a good place to hide something like that suitcase, I'd imagine," Longarm suggested. "I don't reckon you had somebody go through 'em looking for it?"

"I can't tell you whether Carstow had those cars searched or not, Marshal," Forbes replied. "But I'll get the yardmen on it right away."

Nita returned with Longarm's breakfast, and the two men fell silent until she'd put the plate on the table and left.

"There's one thing more I'll ask you to help me with now," Longarm said before turning his attention to the plate of ham and eggs. "I know the Santa Fe's got some kind of connection with Fred Harvey—"

"Nothing official, Marshal," Forbes broke in. "Call it an unwritten understanding that food shipments to the Harvey

Houses along our line get special attention, and that Mr. Harvey can look for us to help him in getting locations for his restaurants and hotels that will be convenient for Santa Fe passengers."

Longarm nodded. "It don't matter to me what your deal is, Mr. Forbes. All I'll ask you to do is drop a hint to the man that runs this place here that if he goes outa his way a little bit to help me on this case, he's helping the Santa Fe."

"I don't see anything wrong with that," Forbes agreed after a moment's thought. "I'll do it on my way out. I don't suppose you'd like to tell me what you've got in mind?"

"I'd just as soon not right now," Longarm replied. "But I ain't going to ask him to do nothing outa line, just sorta look the other way while I work a scheme I figured out."

"I hope your scheme works," Forbes said. "Now I've got to get to work. With Carstow dead, I've got a lot of loose ends that need attention."

After Forbes left, Longarm devoted his attention to his breakfast. He was just pushing his plate aside when the Harvey House manager came to his table.

"I'm Cliff Jackson, Marshal," he said. "Mr. Forbes told me you might have a question to ask me."

"It ain't exactly a question," Longarm replied. "I got a favor to ask of you, though."

"If it's possible to oblige you, I'll certainly do it."

"I need a little bit of help on this case I'm trying to work out. I guess you heard the Santa Fe's lost some property that's real important to 'em?"

"I suppose everybody in Deming knows something that belongs to the Santa Fe's missing, but I don't think anybody knows just what it is," Jackson replied. "I certainly don't."

"What's missing ain't all that much of a secret," Longarm told him. "It's a suitcase with some business papers in it."

"And the Santa Fe's anxious to get them back, I'm sure."

"Real anxious," Longarm nodded. He paused, framing in his mind the best way to present his request. To gain time, he took out a cheroot and lighted it. He went on, "Now, you got a lot of nice young ladies working here."

"Yes. Mr. Harvey insists that they be neat and clean and

that they don't act forward with the patrons," Jackson said.

"But while they're doing their work, I'm sure they hear little bits and pieces of what the folks at the tables are saying," Longarm went on. "Now, all I want is to ask them to make special note of anything they hear that might help me close my case, and tell me what they heard and who said it."

For a moment the restaurant manager sat frowning. Then his face cleared and he said, "We discourage our girls from eavesdropping, Marshal Long. But I can understand how important this might be to you and the Santa Fe. Now, the breakfast rush is just beginning, but it'll be over in an hour or so. If you'd like to come back then and explain what you want our Harvey girls to do, I'll certainly let them help you."

Chapter 12

Longarm stepped forward after Cliff Jackson's introduction and faced the Harvey girls. They stood in a ragged half-circle around him in one of the unfinished rooms off the restaurant. Though none of them bore any specific resemblance to another in terms of build or size or facial features, their uniforms gave them a confusing similarity. He carefully avoided letting his eyes pause on Nita, who stood demurely at the back of the group.

"Well, ladies, I guess you all know who I am, and you're wondering what I got to say to you," he began, then paused as he searched for the right words to use in his explanation. Nods from the girls encouraged him to continue. "Now, Mr. Jackson's told you I need some help on the case I was sent down here on from Denver. I expect all of you have heard about a suitcase that somebody stole from the Santa Fe depot a little while back, and maybe you've figured out that what I'm going to ask you to help me with has got something to do with that suitcase."

Longarm paused again, still seeking the best way to phrase his request, and again some of the Harvey girls nodded. He went on, "The reason why I'm here talking to you is because I got a real big favor I'd like to ask you to do for me. Not just me, but the Santa Fe, too, and that means you ladies, because if it wasn't for the Santa Fe coming here there wouldn't be no Harvey House, either."

For the usually laconic Longarm, his remarks had been a long speech. He paused once more while deciding what he should say next.

One of the Harvey girls asked, "What kind of favor, Marshal?"

"I'm getting to that," he replied. "Now, I don't want you nice young ladies to take what I'm going to say the wrong way,

but I know you can't help it sometimes if you hear what somebody says at a table you're waiting on. What I'm asking you
to do is listen careful if you hear anything about bonds or a
treaty or a suitcase, and then come tell me about it."

"You mean if they say just anything about them?" one of
the girls asked. "Not that they know anything special, or like
that? Because I think most of us have heard the customers
talking about that suitcase being missing."

"I meant just what I said," Longarm replied. "Even a word
or two might be important to me."

"You said 'treaty' a minute ago," another girl said. "What's
that?"

"That's what two countries write down when they make any
kind of a deal," Longarm replied. "I don't know if you've
heard or not, but one of the things in that suitcase was a paper
that tells about a deal Mexico made with our country about
letting our railroads run south of the border."

"Well, I sure haven't heard about anything like that," one
of the girls in the back volunteered. "I guess we've all heard
somebody or other talking about the suitcase, but not much
about what's in it."

"If any of you remember what you've already heard, I'd be
real grateful if you'll tell me," Longarm said. "I'll be staying
in that office car that's on the first siding past the Santa Fe
depot, and if you don't find me there, you can tell me when I
come in to eat."

"We aren't supposed to leave the Harvey House unless Mr.
Jackson gives us permission," another girl said. She turned to
the manager and asked, "What about that, Mr. Jackson? Can
we go tell the marshal right away, if we hear something?"

"It's perfectly all right," Jackson replied. "Just tell me you're
going to see Marshal Long before you leave."

"Even during the dinner or supper rush?" another asked.

"Yes, indeed," he replied. "In fact, if you hear anything at
all, I expect the marshal would want to know it at once."

"I sure would," Longarm agreed. "And if you can remember
anything you've heard folks say about that suitcase these past
few days, I'll stay here till you've had a chance to tell me."

"Do we get anything for telling you?" one of the older girls asked. "Like a reward, I mean."

"So far, the Santa Fe ain't offered a reward, but it sure wouldn't surprise me if they'd pay one," Longarm told her. "In fact, I'll ask my chief to see if he can talk to them about it."

"I guess we've all heard people talking about the suitcase these past few days," one of the girls said. "But all anybody I've heard talking seems to know is that someone took it."

A murmur of agreement rippled through the Harvey girls and as it died down one asked, "Marshal, aren't you going to tell us what else was in the suitcase besides that treaty?"

This was the question Longarm had hoped to avoid, but was sure would be asked. He had his reply ready; it was the strict truth, but sidestepped the value of the missing bonds.

"Just papers that's important to the Santa Fe, but ain't much use to anybody else," he said. "There wasn't any money in it, if that's what you're getting at." When the girl who'd asked the question nodded and turned to say something to the one who stood beside her, Longarm waited for a moment, then said, "Well, I guess that's about all, ladies. Thanks for listening to me, and I sure hope you won't forget about what I been telling you."

Jackson broke the silence that settled over the room after Longarm's last remark. He said, "All right, girls. You know what Marshal Long needs, so try to help him if you can. Now let's all get back to work."

When the Harvey girls began filing out of the room, Nita did not join them. She came up to Longarm and said in a half-whisper, "I don't really have anything to say, but I thought if they saw me talking to you it might encourage the others."

"That's a good idea, Nita," Longarm nodded.

"It didn't seem to do much good," she said, indicating the departing girls. "But I'll do what I can to stir them up. And if any of them says anything interesting to me, I'll pass it on to you. I hope you'll be expecting me tonight?"

"I sure will," he replied. "I'm getting started later than I'd figured, and I need to hurry up and go on out to Carson's place. I oughta be back by suppertime, so come over to the car whenever you can get away."

111

"You know I will," Nita smiled. "Now I'd better go join the others."

Longarm waited a moment after Nita had left, then followed her through the kitchen and out the side door. He'd made good use of the hour he'd had to wait until the Harvey girls could assemble. After renting a horse at the livery stable, he'd checked out of the hotel and moved his scanty luggage—a blanket roll that contained a change of clothes—into the office car.

His horse was waiting at the hitch-rail in front of the Harvey House. Swinging into the saddle, he angled from the railroad tracks through Deming and away from the town. For half a mile the road was well-marked, cut with wagon wheels and thick with hoofprints. Gradually the tracks grew scarce, and the road was virtually unmarked when Longarm reached the spot where it forked. Most of the hoofprints and wheel ruts showed on the right-hand branch, which meandered toward the distant mountain ridges. The other leg stretched as straight as a taut string across the arid land to the west.

Longarm took the fork that led straight ahead, and most of the remaining tracks also vanished after he'd ridden less than a mile. On his right, the distant tip of the Seven Brothers showed green against an almost colorless sky. To his left the land stretched in low, undulating dun-hued waves until it merged with and seemed to become a part of the sky, or the sky part of the land.

Ahead of him the only sign of civilization was the beaten strip of the road he was following, and at long intervals on the prairie beside it the wooden stakes from which tattered, faded red ribbons sagged in the windless morning air.

Them stakes would be the Santa Fe survey, old son, he told himself silently as the livery nag plodded along. *And likely it won't be any more than that if they don't close up that deal they made with the SP. But the way this country looks, about the only reason they'd have for building a railroad here would be to get to someplace where there's rangeland or cropland or towns. It sorta makes a man wonder sometimes if them high railroad muckety-mucks in their fancy offices back East knows what it's really like out here.*

Longarm lighted a cheroot and its thin line of smoke trailed behind him as he rode on. Almost an hour passed before he saw what he'd been looking for: a low-roofed adobe house about a mile off the road, its squat square bulk breaking the otherwise featureless line of the horizon. He reached the thin line of a trail which left the road and led to the house and reined his horse onto it. As he drew nearer he saw a small corral beyond the house, three horses inside the pole enclosure.

Looks like old Sam Carson's at home, all right, he mused as he drew closer to the house. *And chances are he's watching right now and maybe wondering who's come all this way to bother him.*

Longarm had covered almost three-quarters of the distance from the road to the house when its door swung open and a man carrying a rifle came out. He moved slowly, holding the rifle by its muzzle and using it as a cane. One of his legs dragged, and his body bent forward at an unnatural angle as he walked the three or four steps necessary to reach the hitch-rail that stood in front of the house.

Leaning against the rail, he raised the rifle and rested it casually in the crook of his arm. Longarm noticed that the muzzle was not aimed at him, but was in a position to allow for a quick shot.

As the distance between them closed, Longarm could make out details of the man's appearance. Though he'd never encountered Sam Carson before, he'd read his description often enough on Wanted flyers to be sure that he was looking at the notorious old outlaw.

Carson looked to be in his seventies. His thin nose came down in a straight line from bushy white eyebrows and a grizzled white two-day beard sprouted on his wrinkled face. A full moustache drooped down on both sides of his thin lips almost to his chin and his neck sagged in turkey wattles. The few long strands of his hair that remained were brushed straight back, but were so thin that Longarm could see two long, jagged scars on his tanned scalp. His eyes were of a blue so light that they were almost colorless. He wore dark serge trousers and a faded blue shirt that had seen many washings, and soft leather bed-room slippers encased his feet.

"You've come close enough," Carson called when Longarm

was still fifty yards distant. He twitched the rifle the exact amount to allow Longarm to look directly into the black hole of its muzzle. Longarm reined in. Carson went on, "I got just enough water for my own stock, so if that's what you're looking for you can turn around and head back to the road. That nag of yours don't look like it's hurting none, and there's a town about ten miles ahead where you can get all the water you need."

"It ain't water I'm looking for," Longarm replied.

"Same thing goes for grub," Carson told him. "I ain't in the business of feeding every saddle-tramp that passes by. Now, turn that horse and get on your way."

"I didn't come begging," Longarm said. "I'm here to talk."

"I never seen you in my life before now," Carson replied, squinting to examine Longarm more closely. "And I got nothing to say, except tell you again to skeedaddle before I get outa sorts and limber up this Winchester."

"Don't be too previous," Longarm suggested, keeping his voice level. "I didn't swing off the road and ride over here just because I liked the looks of your place. I come here looking for Sam Carson, and if I ain't mistaken, you're him."

Carson did not reply for several moments while he examined Longarm more closely. Finally he said, "I remember faces pretty good, but I don't recall ever seeing yours before."

"I don't reckon you have," Longarm agreed. "Any more'n I've seen yours. That don't keep me from knowing about you."

"You got a name, I guess?"

"Oh, sure. Except it wouldn't mean nothing to you."

"Try me," Carson suggested.

"I'll try the one I'm travelling under now. Custis."

Carson frowned for a moment, then shook his head. "Never heard it before."

"I didn't expect you had. And I damn sure ain't going to give you another one."

"How'd you run across mine?"

"A fellow I talked to in Deming."

"Big fat man? Gambler?" Carson asked.

"You hit first time. I had a little how-to-do with him and his partner. Partner's travelling under the name of Bates."

Carson nodded and lowered his rifle. He said somewhat grudgingly, "They wouldn't've sent you out here if you wasn't all right. Come on inside, Custis. I don't know what brought you here, but I'm willing to listen."

Longarm dismounted, led the horse to the hitch-rail, and tossed the reins over the rail. Using his rifle as a cane again, Carson had taken a step toward the door before turning. He led the way into the house. The room Longarm entered as he followed Carson inside spanned the width of the house. Its walls were adobe, whitewashed, and the ceiling had been whitewashed between its supporting *vigas*. Sunlight from high windows on each side of the doorway flooded into the room and illuminated its spartan furnishings. There was a long, narrow table, a small divan, a leather-upholstered easy chair, and a straight chair. An unholstered Colt lay on the broad arm of the big chair.

Carson settled into the easy chair and motioned for Longarm to sit down in the other. He looked at Longarm closely again and said, "That name you give me didn't ring no bell right off, but it seems like I've heard it someplace."

"Might be you have," Longarm nodded. "I don't expect I'm the only one that answers to it."

"Well, go ahead," the old man said. "What's brought you out here?"

"I told you I was sent," Longarm replied. "But what I'm doing in these parts is something else. I heard about the Santa Fe losing one hell of a big lot of money and I figured I might find a way to get hold of it."

"Did you now?" Carson grinned. "Who'd you hear that from?"

"Oh, I got a whisper up in Colorado and talked to a man in Santa Fe that told me a little bit more."

"You've covered a lot of ground."

"Men in our line of work has to, Carson. You know that a lot better'n I do, seeing you been at it longer."

"I ain't covered no ground for too damn long," the old outlaw grunted. "Got shot up pretty good, and when a man gets old it takes him a while to heal up." When Longarm said nothing, he went on, "Well, Custis, I got some bad news for you. You're halfway right, but you're halfway wrong."

"Meaning what?"

"Meaning that somebody did make a big haul off of the Santa Fe. It wasn't cash, though. It was bonds. And whoever pulled the job taken some papers, too. They must've been pretty important, because I hear over the grapevine that they'd like mighty well to get 'em back."

Covering his surprise by lighting a cigar, Longarm did not reply at once. In spite of his years as a lawman, he still had not been able to solve the mystery of the outlaw grapevine, how news of a major crime circulated so quickly among men on the wrong side of the law. Sam Carson, in his isolated hideaway, obviously knew as much about the theft as Longarm did himself.

"I guess you're sure about that?" he asked.

"Oh, it's a fact," Carson assured him.

"You happen to know how much them bonds might be worth?"

"One hell of a lot, but I ain't found out no real figures."

"Don't you expect the Santa Fe might pay out a pretty good piece of money to get 'em back?"

"You mean you know who's got 'em?"

"Now, if I knew that much, I wouldn't be here, would I?" Longarm asked Carson. "What I was figuring is that you might know more'n I do about where they are now. Was you to know, I imagine I could get 'em and sell 'em back to the Santa Fe, and we'd figure out a split between us."

This time it was Carson who sat quietly, thinking. At last he said, "If I did know, I don't figure I'd need your help, Custis. I still got a little life left in me."

"Oh, I can see that," Longarm nodded. "But it'd be pretty long odds that—" He broke off as he heard the thudding of hoofbeats outside the house.

Carson said quickly, "Don't get upset, Custis. That's my nephew coming back from town. Blade's been staying with me till I can get around good again."

Outside, the drumming hoofbeats stopped. Longarm started to rise, but before he could get to his feet the door burst open and a younger version of Sam Carson came into the room.

"We got to get a move on, Uncle!" he said as he came through the door. "I heard in town that the Santa Fe's brought that son of a bitch Longarm to—" He stopped when he saw Longarm and stood staring.

"Longarm!" Carson growled, his hand reaching for the Colt on the chair arm. "Custis Long! I knew I oughta—"

Longarm had started a dive to the floor the instant he'd heard his name. His sudden, unplanned movement placed him in a situation that made a quick draw of his holstered Colt impossible, but as he hit the floor and rolled toward the wall he raised his hand to his watch-chain and whisked out his derringer.

By the time Longarm reached the wall the stubby little weapon was in his hand, and at such close range it was impossible for him to miss. His first shot sent a slug into Sam Carson. The old man's nephew had been slow to draw. His revolver was only halfway out of its holster when the second slug from the derringer cut him down.

Letting the derringer fall, Longarm whisked out his Colt, even though he could see by then that he would not need it. Sam Carson was sprawled back in the big leather chair, the Colt held loosely in his lifeless fingers. In the rectangle of sunlight that streamed through the open door, the nephew lay in a motionless heap. Longarm got to his feet and looked at the two bodies.

Well, old son, he told himself, *maybe old Sam could've found out about them bonds and maybe he couldn't, but he sure ain't going to be able to help you none now.*

Chapter 13

"So that's the way it stands now, Mr. Forbes," Longarm concluded his account of his visit to Sam Carson's hideout and the gunplay that had resulted in the death of the old outlaw and his nephew.

Longarm and Forbes had eaten a late supper together and were sitting over a final cup of coffee in the Harvey House. The supper hour was over and customers were beginning to trickle out.

"Do you think that Carson or his nephew had anything to do with the murder of Mr. Carstow?" Forbes asked.

Longarm shook his head. "It ain't likely. Sam Carson was an outlaw, but killing without no reason just wasn't his style. Now, if Carstow'd got in Sam's way while he was holding up one of your trains or maybe your depot ticket office, he'd have cut him down without batting an eyelash. Of course, I don't know as much about his nephew as I do about Sam, but I don't see why either one of 'em would've hid out and put a bullet through a window, the way Carstow got killed."

"Have you made any progress in finding out who did kill him?"

"Now, remember, that ain't my case, Mr. Forbes," Longarm reminded the Santa Fe official. "At least, it ain't so far. It's up to the town marshal to handle that shooting."

"Tyler's not doing anything about it, as far as I can see," Forbes said. "Neither he nor his deputy have been around since they came out after you'd reported it to them. I'd still feel better if the matter was in your hands."

"If I find out that there's some connection between Mr. Carstow being shot and them bonds being missing, that'd be something else. But I can't bull in and take it over, the way it stands right now."

"I hate to impose on you, Marshal Long, but you know that Tyler and I don't get along any too well. Do you think you could find out exactly what he's doing?" Forbes asked. "I had a wire from the head office this afternoon, and among other things they asked for a full report on Carstow's murder."

"Well, you know me and Tyler didn't exactly hit it off when I reported that killing to him," Longarm said. "But I'll see if I can find out anything for you."

"I'd appreciate it a lot," Forbes told him. He went on, "Getting back to Carson, I suppose you searched his house before you left?"

"Why, sure. That's what kept me from getting back here a long time ago."

"And found nothing," Forbes went on. His words weren't a question, but a statement.

"There wasn't much to search," Longarm told the Santa Fe man. "A cabinet in the kitchen with some cooking gear in it and a bureau in one of the bedrooms that had two or three pair of longjohns and a few shirts in the drawers. There was a couple of hundred dollars in it, too. The other bedroom didn't have anything in it except a bed and a chair."

"No letters or papers of any sort?"

"You got to understand something about outlaws, Mr. Forbes," Longarm said. "As a general rule, they don't get no letters. When an outlaw's wanted real bad, he'll dive into a hidey-hole someplace and pull the hole closed behind him. Even if he's got kinfolks or a wife, he don't want them writing him letters, because lawmen and bounty hunters can trace 'em."

"Yes, that makes sense," Forbes nodded. "I just hadn't thought about it before. You arranged for the bodies to be buried, I guess?"

"Oh, sure. There not being any sheriff around, I told the local undertaker to go out and put 'em away. He'll send his bill to the territorial marshal in Santa Fe."

"We're no further ahead in finding the missing bonds than we were, then," Forbes said, discouragement showing in his voice.

"Well, I wouldn't say that," Longarm replied. "There's still some things I need to follow up on."

"How much time is it going to take you to do that, Marshal Long?"

"Not much way of saying," Longarm admitted. "I'm running sorta behind. That dustup with Sam Carson kept me away from town all day, and I ain't heard from none of the Harvey girls yet. They might come up with some leads that'll help out."

"I'm not just being curious," Forbes went on. "Some of the big brass from the Chicago office are coming out here in a few days, and things are going to be pretty uncomfortable for me if I can't report some kind of progress in finding that suitcase."

"About all I can do is keep pushing," Longarm told him. "And I sure don't aim to ease up none." He pushed his coffee cup away and went on, "There's one or two of these Harvey girls that might've stumbled onto something that'll help, and I need to talk to them. The place ain't all that busy now, so maybe I can get my business finished instead of waiting till they close."

Longarm lingered at the cashier's stand after he and Forbes had paid their checks and the Santa Fe man had departed. He told Cliff Jackson, "I got a few things I'd like to ask one of your young ladies about, and seeing as the place ain't so crowded now, I figure to wait and talk to her, if you don't mind."

"Of course I don't, Marshal. Which one is it?"

"Her name's Janet. I seen all their names on their dresses this morning, but they outnumbered me pretty good, and I can't just recall her face."

Jackson glanced around at the few tables still occupied and said, "That's Janet, clearing that table in the corner. There won't be anything for her to do; we'll be closing soon. Why don't you just go over and talk to her now?"

Janet was a small, pert girl with a coil of red hair showing above her black-trimmed white headband. She looked around when Longarm walked up and said, "I thought I saw you leave with Mr. Forbes, Marshal."

"I guess I seen you about the same time and remembered that I wanted to ask you one or two questions," Longarm replied. "I talked to Mr. Jackson, and he said it'd be all right."

"Questions about what?"

120

"A night or so ago, you was waiting on the town marshal and his deputy," Longarm replied. "I understand they was talking about burying something and bones and I don't know what all else. I got to wondering if it might have something to do with what I was explaining to you girls this morning."

"Nita must've told you about that," Janet said. "I don't remember mentioning it to anybody else."

"I guess she must've," Longarm agreed. "Anyhow, it stuck in my mind and I figured I better find out about it from you."

"I really didn't hear very much," she frowned. "And none of it made any sense. I guess that's why it stuck in my mind."

"Why don't you just start out and tell me everything you heard 'em say," he suggested. "Maybe between us we can figure it all out."

Janet nodded. "The first thing that I remember was Marshal Tyler saying how concerned he was about the way his bones were bothering him."

Longarm frowned. "You're certain that Tyler was talking about rheumatism, are you? It seems to me like he's a mite too young a man to be bothered with something like that."

"Well, my mother had rheumatism so bad that she was always worrying about her bones aching, and I guess that's what started me paying attention to what he was talking about. You know, I don't usually even hear much of what my customers are saying, unless they're giving me their order or asking me for water or more coffee or something like that."

"Sure, I understand," Longarm nodded.

"It couldn't've been anything else, could it? What else but rheumatism makes your bones ache, Marshal Long?"

"Nothing I know of," he said. "What did the deputy say when the marshal told him that?"

"I left their table just when Mr. Peters was starting to answer him. It was a few minutes before I got back with a pitcher of gravy for their mashed potatoes," Janet went on. "And by then they'd started talking about how bad the coyotes had been out on the desert this past summer."

"They didn't say anything else about bones, then?"

Janet shook her head. "No. Just how there'd be a lot more coyotes coming down from the mountains with winter so close, and time for it to start snowing up in the high country. You know, the mountains start just a little ways to the north."

"It didn't strike you as being a little bit funny that the town marshal and his deputy'd be interested in coyotes?" Longarm frowned.

"Not a bit, Marshal Long. All the cattle ranchers come to town from the foothills and talk about coyotes getting at their stock. You'd be surprised how much we hear about them."

"I guess maybe I would. Well, go on. What did they say about the coyotes?"

"Nothing except how they chewed up a steer's carcass right down to the bones, and there wasn't enough left of it for anybody to tell what it had been before the coyotes got at it."

"Is that all they talked about the rest of the time they was in here?" he asked.

"It must've been, because the only thing else I remember hearing them say was later on, when they got to talking about how the Santa Fe was having trouble keeping the hoboes out of those old bunkhouse cars in their yards."

"What'd they have to say about that?"

"I was away for a minute right then, but when I got back Mr. Tyler was telling his deputy that he'd tried to get the railroad to move the bunkhouse cars someplace else, and what they ought to do was just to burn them up."

Longarm frowned thoughtfully when he heard Janet's answer. He was silent for a moment before he asked, "Did it sound to you like Tyler was saying him and the deputy oughta do that?"

"Why . . ." Janet hesitated, then shook her head and said, "I just don't know whether Mr. Tyler meant that the Santa Fe ought to do the burning or whether him and Mr. Peters ought to. To tell you the truth, Marshal Long, I wasn't paying all that much attention. You know, people are always complaining about things, and after a while you just don't really think about what they mean."

"Did they say anything else, later on?"

"Oh, they talked a little bit about how winter was going to bring more hoboes into town pretty soon, when it got cold up around Trinidad and Albuquerque and Santa Fe. I remember

122

one of them saying something about the hoboes not being missed if they didn't show up, or something like that."

"But all during the time they was eating dinner, Tyler nor Peters neither one said a thing about that suitcase I'm looking for?"

"If they did, I didn't hear them."

Longarm could tell that Janet was getting restless now, and decided that since all the information he'd gotten from her thus far was of little help to him, there was small likelihood he'd do any better by further questioning.

"Well, I do thank you, Janet," he said. "You've been real helpful, and I appreciate it. Just remember, if you hear anything about that missing suitcase, be sure to tell me."

"I won't forget," she promised. "And neither will the other girls. We've all been talking about how nice you are, and how exciting it is to be doing something like you asked us to."

As Longarm's eyes followed Janet walking away, he saw Nita watching him from the opposite side of the room. Her lips moved slowly, forming a silent message: "Later." He nodded in reply before leaving the Harvey House and going to the car that had been Carstow's office and living quarters.

His saddlebags and bedroll still lay in the middle of the office floor where he'd dropped them when he arrived from the hotel, and his rifle was leaning in the corner where he'd left it after returning from his visit to Sam Carson's place. The bottle of Tom Moore sat on the table, and as soon as he'd pulled down the window shades, Longarm took a swallow before carrying his bedroll and saddlebags into the sleeping compartment where he spread his blankets on the narrow bed.

Taking the pouch containing his gun-cleaning gear from the saddlebags, he returned to the office compartment, slipped his derringer out of his vest pocket, and laid it on the table, then drew his Colt and laid it beside them. Lighting a fresh cheroot, he sat down, swallowed another sip of the rye whiskey, and picked up the derringer. He'd cleaned and reloaded it and was starting to clean the Colt when the door opened and Nita slipped in.

"You're certainly a lot more trusting than I'd be," she commented as she closed the door and locked it.

"If you'll look, you'll see I ain't as careless as you might think," he replied, indicating the derringer. "I didn't unload the Colt before I had my backup cleaned and loaded."

"I should've known you'd think of that," Nita smiled, hanging her cloak on the hook beside the door. "I saw you talking to Janet. Did she have anything helpful to tell you?"

"As best I could make out, it was just about what you'd heard her say," Longarm answered. "What all she'd heard Tyler and Peters gabbing about, which wasn't too much help."

"They weren't talking about the suitcase, then?"

Longarm shook his head. "And it wasn't because she forgot it, because I asked her special. She said they were complaining about the hoboes and coyotes coming here where it's warm now that winter's hitting in the mountain country. And she'd heard them say something about how the Santa Fe oughta burn them bunkhouse cars that're on the sidings here in the yards because the drifters sleep in 'em."

"It looks like I was wrong about us overhearing things you could use, then," Nita said. "I'm sorry, Longarm."

"Oh, there wasn't a thing wrong with your scheme, Nita. I ain't giving up."

"Even if all you hear about is hoboes and bones?"

"Even if—" Longarm stopped short, a thoughtful frown crinkling his brow.

"What's the matter?" Nita asked as the seconds ticked away and he still remained silent. "Did you think of something else, or was it something I said?"

"Part of both, maybe," Longarm replied.

"Are you going to tell me about it? Or do you need to think it through some more?"

"I ain't sure."

"Suppose you tell me," she suggested. "Maybe I can help you connect up whatever it is."

"Maybe you can," he said. "The other day, right after I got in, Forbes asked me if I'd mind telling the town marshal that Carstow'd been shot. Seems like Tyler's sorta down on the Santa Fe."

"That's not unusual," Nita commented. "Town constables and sheriffs almost always resent outsiders, and that includes railroad police and Pinkerton people. I've run into that, and so have a lot of others at the agency."

"Oh, I run into it myself," Longarm nodded. "Matter of fact, Tyler wasn't exactly glad to see me. But that's neither here nor there. What I started out to say was that when I was in his office the other day, his deputy brought in a hobo, one that Tyler'd told him to run outa town, get rid of him."

"And the deputy hadn't done it?"

"No. It seems like the hobo wanted to tell Tyler thanks for buying him a feed before he was tossed out, so the deputy had brought him back to the office."

"From what I've seen of Tyler, he's not exactly the kind who'd be buying meals for bindle-stiffs," Nita commented.

"That's what the barkeep in the saloon where I stopped for a drink said, too, when I mentioned it. As a matter of fact, the barkeep said he knew for a fact that Tyler didn't have one smidgen of use for hoboes."

Nita shook her head and said, "I still don't see how this has anything to do with . . . well, with our case."

"I ain't sure it does, except for two things. Tyler spent a lot of time telling me how soft-hearted he is about hoboes."

"Maybe he is," she suggested.

"And maybe he was lying."

"What makes you think so?"

"Because the hobo called himself Bones Jones."

"Bones Jo—" Nita began, and stopped short. "You think that when Janet overheard Tyler and Peters talking about bones, they might have been talking about the hobo?"

"I'm thinking about that and something more. I got an idea she just thought them two was talking about coyotes coming down from the mountains for the winter. You know anything much about coyotes, Nita?"

"Only that they're a lot like wolves and live in the desert in this part of the country."

"Coyotes are scavengers," Longarm said thoughtfully. "They eat just about anything that's dead."

Now it was Nita who frowned and shook her head. "I still don't follow what you're thinking about," she said.

"Let me put it to you this way," Longarm suggested. "Just

suppose that when Tyler and Peters was talking about coyotes and Janet thought all they meant was coyotes gnawing on any kind of bones, they was really talking about Bones Jones. What'd that bring you up to thinking next?"

Nita replied unhesitatingly, "That Bones Jones was dead, of course."

No sooner were the words out of her mouth than her eyes widened and she went on, "If he's dead, and Tyler had told Peters to get rid of him, that could mean Peters killed him."

"And didn't have time to bury him," Longarm agreed. "What Peters might've been saying was that they didn't need to worry because the coyotes would eat Bones Jones up, so nobody could tell who he was or that he'd got killed, much less who killed him."

Nita shuddered. "It's not a thing I like to think about, but your theory hangs together."

"It makes a lot more sense when you figure what else Janet thought she'd heard 'em say, about the Santa Fe burning them old bunkhouse cars," Longarm went on. "It was broad daylight when Peters took Bones Jones outa the marshal's office. Now, was I going to take a man out and shoot him, I sure wouldn't do it out on the open prairie in broad daylight."

"Of course not. If you were going to commit a murder, you'd find a place where nobody could see you."

Longarm nodded. "Like one of the old bunkhouse cars. There's a whole bunch of 'em on sidings here in the yards. And it just might be that Carstow saw something also, which is why he got shot too. I figure the hobo did something for Tyler and Peters, and maybe Carstow saw their transaction. So first they got rid of the Santa Fe superintendent and then they got rid of the hobo, when he was through being useful to 'em."

"We'll have to search the cars, of course," Nita said.

"Not we, Nita. Me," Longarm told her. "And not tonight, tomorrow."

"I was hoping you'd say that," she said. "Because I think from the sample you gave me last night, I'd like a full serving tonight. Come on, Longarm. Let's go to bed!"

Chapter 14

"It appears to me that you're not quite yourself this morning, Marshal Long," Forbes commented as he and Longarm sat at breakfast in the Harvey House. "Is there something about this case that's bothering you?"

"Well, I guess every case I go out on bothers me one way or another," Longarm replied. "But maybe it's just because I had a real busy morning and ain't got a thing to show for it."

"A sleepless night, then?" Forbes suggested.

"I didn't have much sleep, that's a fact," Longarm said.

He did not bother to tell Forbes the reason was that Nita had been with him. Through the hours of darkness they'd stayed locked together in amorous embraces until the first gray hint of dawnlight creeping in around the drawn window shades of the office car's small bedroom warned them the night was over.

After she had dressed hurriedly and left for the Harvey House, Longarm had begun thinking about their deductions involving Tyler and Peters, and the new ideas these had created had kept him wide awake until sunup.

Longarm went on, "I had a new idea or two about some things I might've been overlooking, so I got up early and ever since then I been searching through them bunkhouse cars you got on the sidings out in the yards."

"I'd say you're just tired, then," Forbes told him.

"Maybe that's it," Longarm agreed. "The way them cars is cut up inside, into three stacks of bunks, it ain't right easy to go through 'em."

"I'm sure they're in pretty bad shape," Forbes said. "I don't imagine they were cleaned when they were sidetracked. All of us expected the job to start up again after a few days. None of us realized they'd still be standing there after two years."

"I'd say they ain't been cleaned since they was put to use,"

Longarm replied. "They got all kinds of trash in 'em, and they stink like hell to boot. I had to stick my head out every now and then for a breath of fresh air."

"Yes, I can see where searching twenty of them would be a big job," Forbes nodded.

"It was a job, all right. But you're wrong about there being twenty of them cars. There ain't but nineteen."

"You must've miscounted," Forbes frowned. "I've been spending a lot of time going through our office records, because that bunch of high brass from Chicago is due to get here in the next few days, and you never know what kind of questions those collar people from the head office will ask."

"I ain't questioning what your office papers shows, but clerks make mistakes, specially on a big job like pushing new tracks," Longarm pointed out. "If the records in your office show you're supposed to have twenty of them cars, you better check up on 'em."

"I certainly will," Forbes replied. "In fact, I'll do it right now. I'm ready to go back to my car anyhow."

"Well, I ain't got nothing better to do for a few minutes, so I'll just walk back with you and see what you find out. Not that it makes much difference to me, because if I'm right it'd be up to the Santa Fe's own police to find out why there's only nineteen cars instead of twenty. But I got to admit you got my curiosity perked up."

Forbes's office car was a twin to the one in which Longarm was staying. It had a large front compartment fitted to accommodate a table-desk, and its sides were covered with shelves and cubbyholes piled high with stacks of papers and ledgers. Forbes took down a ledger and opened it on the table. He leafed through it and finally stopped at a much-marked-up page.

"This rolling stock book has the record of every car that's been put on this job," he said as he ran a finger down the columns. "From the time they left our shops until now. Here, Marshal, you can look for yourself. You'll see there were twenty-four bunkhouse cars to start with. Three were wrecked and one burned up. Four from twenty-four leaves twenty, or else I wasn't taught to add and subtract correctly."

"Like I told you, I ain't arguing with your books," Longarm

said after glancing at the page. "All I know is that you only got nineteen cars on them sidings. You feel like walking out to count 'em?"

"I'll have to," Forbes replied. "Let's take a look."

Slogging over the loose gravel that covered the areas between the maze of tracks and switches, the two men walked to the sidings where the bunkhouse cars stood on spurs. Counting them was a job of less than a minute. When they'd finished their tally, Forbes shook his head, a frown on his face.

"You were right, Marshal Long," he admitted. "Nineteen, just as you said."

Longarm was not a man to say "I told you so." He nodded at Forbes and said, "Well, I guess you got the job of finding out what happened to the car that's missing."

"I'm afraid I have," Forbes agreed. "And I don't know how familiar you are with railroads, Marshal, but there's something about a missing piece of rolling stock that seems to drive the accounting people crazy. They take out after that missing piece like a pack of hounds chasing down a rabbit."

"Maybe what I'm thinking ain't right down the line with your railroad rules," Longarm said. "But couldn't you just change them figures in your books to show you only got nineteen cars?"

Forbes shook his head. "There are duplicates of those ledger pages in the division shops in Albuquerque and the main office in Chicago. I don't think I could get away with it."

"Well, I sure wouldn't want to advise anybody to play fast and loose with the truth, Mr. Forbes, but on something like this I might be tempted to give it a try."

"I don't think so. I remember what happened to a construction superintendent who tried to beat the accounting system on the Northern back when I first got into railroading. One of his crews let a handcar run off the rails at a bridgehead and fall into a river. Instead of reporting it lost, he got a crew together and assembled another handcar out of the spare parts they had on the job for replacements."

"That sounds like good thinking," Longarm said with a grin.

"It wasn't. The river had gone down when the wipe-up crew came along. They could see the handcar upended in the river, so they pulled it out and put it back into service. Of course the next rolling-stock inventory showed the job had a handcar too many. The accounting department started investigating, and when they found out what had happened, all hell broke loose."

"What happened to the man that made up the extra handcar?"

"Oh, he was fired and blacklisted. He couldn't get another railroad job for the rest of his life. I don't want something like that to happen to me."

"I can see how you'd feel," Longarm said. "What're you aiming to do, then?"

"Before I do anything else, I'll walk over to the yard boss's shanty and see if he's got an explanation."

"Well, if you don't mind, I'll go along." As he walked back across the tracks with Forbes, Longarm added, "I sorta got an interest in them bunkhouse cars. They've popped up in my case a time or two."

"Have they now?" Forbes asked. "In what way?"

"I ain't real sure I could explain, Mr. Forbes. It's more of a hunch than anything else."

They took a few more steps in silence before Forbes said, "You know, Marshal, in the job I had before Carstow died, I was on a first-name basis with just about everybody, and I feel a bit uncomfortable being called 'Mister.' Do you mind just making it 'George?'"

"Not a bit. I'm the same way. I got a sorta nickname that most folks calls me. It's Longarm."

"Good," Forbes nodded as they reached the little shanty used by the yard boss. "Now, let's see what Beeker has to say about that missing bunkhouse car."

When Longarm and Forbes heard Beeker's explanation, the Santa Fe man gave a short snort of relief.

"Why sure, I know where that other bunkhouse car is, George. It's propped up on blocks about three miles west of town, on the old survey line."

"How the devil did it get there?"

"Why, Mr. Carstow had it hauled there," Beeker said. "He wanted it ready for the track gang that'd be building back this way to switch onto the main line."

"And it never was used?"

"Not after the new survey was finished. It was way off the new main line. Why?"

"According to the books in the office, it should be here in the yards, with the other bunkhouse cars," Forbes replied.

"Well, that ain't my fault," Beeker said. "Right after the new survey was finished, I told Mr. Carstow we oughta get it back here and put trucks under it again. He kept saying we'd do it, but just never did get around to it."

"Then the car's still standing out there?" Forbes asked.

"Far as I know it is," Beeker replied. "To tell you the truth, we got so busy shutting down the construction job that I sorta forgot about it."

"When did you look at it last?" Forbes frowned.

"Well, now, I couldn't put a month or day to it, but it's been a while. It had already got to be a hangout for hoboes and riffraff, so I don't guess it'd be in very good shape, but I'd imagine it's still there."

As Longarm had listened to the conversation between Forbes and the yard boss, some of the remarks reported by Janet that she'd overheard made by Buck Tyler and his deputy had taken on a new meaning.

He said to Forbes, "Now that you've found out where that car is, I guess you can quit worrying, George. Tell you what, I'll saddle up and mosey out to where it is. I'll tell you what it's like next time I see you."

"If you don't mind waiting until I can go over to the stable and get my horse, I'll go with you," Forbes replied. "I know exactly where the old line survey ran, so it might save you some time. Besides, I'd like to look at that car myself."

A half-hour ride from Deming brought Longarm and Forbes to the long-abandoned bunkhouse car. They did not see it until they were almost on it because the car had been set on blocks placed in the shelter of a little hollow that stood a hundred yards from the line marked by the few survey stakes that still remained.

They reined up beside the car, in an area marked by the ashes of small fires long dead and littered with bits of debris: three or four unmatched old shoes warped by the desert sun, the shreds of a felt hat reduced to fuzzy blobs, some short

131

twisted strips of leather belting and tag ends of fraying rope, several tangles of heavy string, strips of ragged weatherbeaten cloth.

As they dismounted and walked toward the car their noses were assailed a dozen paces away by the odors trickling from the square openings that had once been windows, the gagging stench of excrement and dried urine, the sour smell of ancient sweat.

"I don't know that I'm anxious to go inside," Forbes said as they reached the doorless rectangle at the end of the car. "I can imagine what it's like from what we smell out here."

"Suit yourself," Longarm replied. "I got to go in myself and take a quick look-see. If you don't feel like going in, I'll tell you what it's like."

"No, I'll go along with you," Forbes told him. "It's really my job to find out."

Although the cast-iron steps at the end of the car had been partly wrenched away from the vestibule, they were still sturdy enough to mount. Longarm swung up them easily with his long legs and went inside. In spite of the triple rows of windows, the inside of the car was dim after the dazzling light of the desert sun outside, and for a moment he stood blinking while his eyes adjusted to the suddenly lowered level of light. The stench in the car's interior was almost overpowering, but it had no overtones of the unmistakable odor of rotting human flesh.

Longarm's eyes adjusted and he could see that the car's interior had been totally wrecked. The tiers of bunks which once had risen three-high on both sides had been torn out. Longarm remembered the ash heaps dotting the ground outside and understood where the wood from the bunks had gone.

Oddly, the car's floor was relatively uncluttered. There were some small heaps of rags, and clean-stripped bones were fairly numerous, but for the most part the floor was clear. A scraping from outside told Longarm that George Forbes had finally conquered his reluctance to come inside. Then the doorway darkened and Forbes picked his way slowly to Longarm's side.

"It's not as bad as I was afraid it might be," he remarked, straining his eyes in the dimness as he surveyed the cavernous interior. "At least the floor and walls are still left, and the shop

132

can build new bunks pretty easily. That won't take the smell out, of course."

"You're lucky the hoboes ain't started on the walls yet," Longarm told him.

"These are double-walled cars," Forbes said. "Tongue-and-groove run vertically outside and shiplap angled at forty-five degrees inside, triple-nailed, with bolts around all the windows. They're built to last, and I doubt that the bums who've been using this one had the tools they'd need to tear it apart."

"That won't stop 'em from trying when they need a fire to cook whatever they've managed to beg for a meal," Longarm commented. He started walking slowly to the far end of the car, his sharp eyes darting over the bits of debris strewing the floor.

"You act like you're looking for something special," Forbes said. "I've got an idea it's not just idle curiosity that made you decide to examine this car."

"Well, I don't know exactly what I'm looking for," Longarm replied. "The minute we reined in, I could smell that what I figured I might find out here wasn't around, but as long as I'm here, I figured I might as well give it a good going-over."

"I've seen all I need to," Forbes went on. "I'll wait for you outside, if you don't mind. This stink turns my stomach."

"You go ahead, George," Longarm said. "I'll walk down the car and come out the other end."

Longarm started walking slowly along the length of the car. Forbes turned to go outside. He'd reached the door just as Longarm, near the center of the car now, exhaled a satisfied grunt and bent to pick something up from the floor.

Stopping just inside the door, Forbes asked, "Don't tell me you've found what you were looking for?"

"Like I said, I didn't know what to look for, or anything much else," Longarm replied. "But I got to admit I sure found something real interesting."

Forbes's curiosity drew him back in spite of the smell. He looked at the black-and-white checked woolen cap with a broken bill that Longarm was holding and said, "That doesn't look like much, Longarm. It's just an old worn-out cap some hobo's thrown away. I can't say I blame him, either."

"I grant you it ain't such a much," Longarm agreed. "But that don't mean it ain't important."

"I don't see how it could be," Forbes frowned.

For a moment Longarm did not reply. Then he said, "George, you know I figure you got damn near as much interest in this case as I have."

"More, I'd say. It's just another job for you, but I've spent a good part of my life climbing up to the job I've got with the Santa Fe, and I want to keep it, maybe even advance a bit further. Just exactly what are you getting at?"

"Well, it's too much of a long story to tell you all of it right now, but I seen this cap before."

"If you've seen it once, I don't doubt that you'd be sure to recognize it," Forbes said when Longarm paused. "There can't be too many caps like that around here. I've seen one or two like it back East, though, and I'd say it's imported from England, and it was very expensive when it was new."

"I recognize it, all right," Longarm replied. "The first day I got here. Remember, you asked me to stop by the town marshal's office when I went into Deming, and report that Mr. Carstow'd been killed?"

"Of course I remember," Forbes replied. "But what's that cap got to do with it?"

"It's a long story, and I'd rather tell you when we get outside, where we can breathe some fresh air. Go on out. I'll be there soon as I look all the way to the end of the car, just in case there's something else down that way."

Carrying the cap, Longarm resumed his slow walk along the center of the car. Forbes reached the door and stepped onto the vestibule.

A rifle cracked sharply and a bullet thunked into the side of the car. Almost at once, a second shot followed the first. Forbes staggered back through the doorway, bending as he moved, and fell to the floor.

Longarm had drawn his Colt as the first shot split the air, and was moving to the nearest window opening when the second sounded. He glanced through the window hole, but saw nothing except the barren slope of the little hollow in which the bunkhouse car rested. He took three long steps to the opposite side and another window hole.

Above the top rim of the hollow he saw the head and shoulders of a horseman on the downslope beyond the rim of the hollow. Longarm's quick shot lifted the rider's hat off, but before he could trigger a second shot his target had vanished. He stood at the window for a moment, but the attacker did not reappear.

Having no intention of wasting good lead on the empty air, Longarm hurried to the end of the car where Forbes lay. He dropped to one knee beside the railroader.

"Are you hit bad?" Longarm asked, scrutinizing Forbes for signs of a wound and seeing no blood.

"I—I don't think so. I got hit in my arm, but the bullet knocked me down."

Longarm holstered his Colt. The bushwhacker who'd fired the shot was long gone by now, and he had the wounded Forbes to look after. He asked, "Can you sit up?"

"I guess so," Forbes replied, bringing himself to a sitting position with Longarm's help.

"Let's get your coat off and have a look," Longarm said, pulling the coat's lapels apart and down.

He looked at the bloodstain spreading on the sleeve of his companion's shirt. It was a steady spread, not the pulsing flow that would have been gushing if the big subclavian artery running down inside the biceps had been hit.

"It ain't too bad," Longarm assured Forbes, who was staring down at his bloody shirtsleeve.

His voice showing his astonishment, Forbes said, "Funny, it doesn't hurt at all, but I can see I'm bleeding."

"Sure," Longarm told him, reaching into his hip pocket for the big bandana handkerchief he carried there. "The bullet just went through that muscle in your arm without touching bone. You might not think so, George, but you're a lucky man. Now, sit still while I fix you up, and we'll get into town and find you a doctor. Then I'll go and get the son of a bitch that shot you!"

Chapter 15

Forbes looked up at Longarm, amazement spreading over his face and his voice showing his surprise. He said, "That sounds like you know who shot me!"

"Maybe I do. I didn't get a good enough look at him to be sure, though," Longarm replied as he finished removing Forbes's coat and tossed it aside. "But that ain't here nor there. Let's take a look at that arm of yours."

While Longarm was busy working at Forbes's shirt, the Santa Fe man asked, "Don't you think you'd better tell me who it is you suspect of trying to kill us?"

"Not right this minute, George," Longarm replied. "Even if I got a pretty good hunch who it could've been, I'm still a long way from being downright certain." By now he had taken off Forbes's stiff collar and unbuttoned the top of the shirt far enough to pull it down to expose his wounded arm. He went on, "You oughta know that having a hunch and being able to prove it's right are two different things."

Longarm fell silent while he examined the wound. A small black-rimmed hole showed in the skin on the railroader's upper arm, just below his armpit. Small drops of blood were slowly oozing from the hole and running down the arm. By leaning forward Longarm could see the exit wound, and he scrutinized it closely. He saw a small but steady stream of blood flowing from its ragged edges and trickling down to drip off Forbes's elbow. He folded the bandana into a triangle and rolled the triangle to make a strip, then wrapped it tightly in a double twist around the wound.

"I get the idea you've done this before," Forbes said.

His head was twisted around to watch what Longarm was doing and he forced the words through his clenched teeth as Longarm knotted the ends of the improvised bandage.

"More'n once. Only some of the men I tried to help ain't been as lucky," Longarm told him.

He'd had enough experience with bullet wounds to know the need to keep their conversation flowing, drawing Forbes's attention from the wound. In a very short time, he knew, the arm would hurt and would begin to swell and throb.

Longarm went on, "Now, you didn't get bad hurt, this ain't much more'n a scratch, George."

"It looks like a pretty big scratch to me," Forbes said ruefully. "There sure was a lot of blood coming from it before you got that bandage on."

"It looks a lot worse'n it is," Longarm assured him. "The slug didn't hit no bone, so it didn't spread out and tear your arm up, and it didn't go in far enough back to cut that big vein in your arm."

"I guess I've got something to be thankful for, then."

"You sure have. All the same, we got to start back to town soon as we can mount up, and get you to a doctor. I done the best I can with what we got."

"You've done pretty well, Longarm. I'm grateful. But I know you're not a doctor."

"Well, he'll likely tell you just about what I did. But all I can do is sorta make shift, and the doctor can put some permanganate on that hole to make it scab over and stop bleeding, then fix up a real bandage for you."

"It's beginning to hurt now," Forbes admitted.

"Sure. It's bound to," Longarm said, getting to his feet. He bent forward to help Forbes up. "Now let me give you a hand up—"

Alerted by an almost inaudible scraping of boot soles on hard ground, Longarm suddenly broke off and dropped flat on the vestibule platform, pulling Forbes down with him. A rifle barked and the slug cut the air above the heads of the two men.

Grabbing his companion by the shoulders, Longarm scuttled backward into the car, dragging Forbes with him as a second shot rang out and the bullet ripped a long strip of splinters along the platform's floor.

Lowering Forbes carefully after they were safely inside the car, Longarm stepped back to the door. As he moved, he drew his Colt again and held it ready while he sheltered himself behind the wall and peered around the edge of the opening. His field of view was very limited and he saw no signs of the man who was attacking them.

"I didn't figure that son of a bitch'd have the guts to come back," Longarm remarked over his shoulder. "But it looks like he's dead set on finishing us off."

"Why would he be after us?" Forbes asked.

"My guess is that he's after me, and you're just catching it because you're here," Longarm said, still trying to see the attacker.

"But we didn't see anybody on the way here. There wasn't anybody around when we rode up."

"Likely we got here before he did." Longarm did not take his eyes off the rim of the hollow as he replied.

Forbes's puzzlement showed in his voice as he said, "I still don't understand what you're getting at, but I know this isn't the time for explanations. What are we going to do?"

"Wait a while," Longarm replied tersely.

"And just let him keep shooting at us?"

"Well, the way I see it, there ain't but two things that fellow out there can do. He can come in after us, or he can give up and scoot."

"We ought to be all right as long as we stay in the car," Forbes observed. "I don't know much about guns, but none of the bullets that've hit the wall have come through that double layer of boards."

"It ain't likely they will," Longarm agreed. "And it won't take that fellow outside much longer to figure it out. You think you'll be all right by yourself for a minute or two, George?"

"Of course. My arm's sore and my shoulder's getting stiff, but I don't need you to look after me."

"Good," Longarm nodded. "I just thought about one more thing he can do that'd put us in a little bit worse pickle than we are now, and I aim to have another try at him before he thinks about it, too."

"What's that?" Forbes frowned.

"He could shoot our horses. It ain't all that far back to Deming, but I ain't hankering to hoof it. And I'd as soon get

138

there the same time he does, or a little bit before, if we can manage it."

"What do you want me to do?" Forbes asked.

Before Longarm could reply, the rifleman holding them fixed in the bunkhouse car fired again. Longarm could tell that the sniper had changed position, for the rifle slug whistled through the door opening inches from his face, passed above the floor where Forbes was lying, and tore a line of splinters from the far wall of the car before thudding into its far end.

"You just stay here and—" Longarm began, then stopped and said, "Wait a minute." He took out his derringer and freed it from his watch-chain. "There's only two loads in this, but that oughta be enough."

"You want me to shoot the fellow if you flush him out?" the railroader asked. He shook his head. "I don't know a thing about guns, Longarm."

"You don't need to. A slug outa this little thing don't carry much farther than a man can spit, but that don't make no nevermind."

"How do I aim it? And where?"

"You don't have to worry about aiming, which is a good thing, because I misdoubt you'll see anything to aim at."

"Tell me what to do, then. I'll do my best," Forbes said.

"All you got to do is just point this derringer anyplace out the door and pull the trigger once, then wait about a minute and let off the second barrel."

"I think I see what you're planning," Forbes nodded. "And I sure can do that much to help. But don't I have to cock this gun or something?"

"It's already cocked," Longarm replied, handing Forbes the derringer. "This little button on the side's the safety. Just push it down before you pull the trigger for the first shot. Then all you got to do to let off the other barrel is pull the trigger again."

"I ought to be able to manage that. I don't guess there's any danger I'll hit you, is there?"

"Not a bit. I'm going out the other end of the car and see if I can get my Winchester outa my saddle scabbard. That'll sorta even things up with that bastard out there."

Crawling on his hands and knees to keep below the bottom

of the lowest window openings, Longarm started for the opposite end of the car. The sniper's rifle cracked again before he reached the door opening and the slug whistled as it passed above him to thunk into the end wall. Then he heard the flat muted clap of the derringer as Forbes fired its first barrel.

Snaking belly-down through the door, Longarm half-slid, half-fell down the vestibule steps to the ground. He rolled under the car to the horses, which were still standing near the end of the car from which he'd emerged, and pulled his Winchester from his saddle scabbard. He was just starting around the end of the car when hoofbeats drummed from the opposite side of the hollow.

Abandoning caution, Longarm raced along the side of the bunkhouse car and up the sloping embankment. He saw the sniper outlined sharply by the declining sun. The man was bending low over the neck of his galloping horse and was already a good five hundred yards distant.

Shouldering his rifle, Longarm took a bead on the retreating rider. He found the man in his sights for a split second and squeezed off a shot, but by the time the Winchester's sharp crack broke the air the horseman was too distant for a sure shot. The fleeing gunman kept his nag at a gallop, and Longarm ran back to his own mount. Swinging into the saddle, he kicked the horse into motion, up the hollow's sloping side and into the desert in pursuit.

For a few minutes after he'd started, helped by the long downslope that stretched away from the hollow, Longarm gained on his quarry. The man ahead was galloping north rather than east toward Deming. Ahead the hillocks of the rolling prairie were broken by a long sandstone ridge, its steep sides reddish against the wide, rolling dun-hued stretch of sandy soil that still separated Longarm from the fleeing gunman.

Once, the man ahead looked back, but all that Longarm could make out with the sun in his eyes was a light blurred outline of his face against the darker ocher of the ridge. The distance between them was still too great for him to make out any of the gunman's features.

Reining in, Longarm raised his rifle and swung its muzzle along the course of the fleeing rider. He waited until he caught him in the rifle's sights again, then led his target a short distance before squeezing off another shot. The range was still too great, for the slug from the Winchester kicked up a spurt of soil a few yards short of the rider.

Longarm resumed his pursuit. The man ahead had closed the distance between him and the sandstone outcrop by now and was riding parallel to its upthrust face. Seeing his intention, Longarm changed his course to a longer angle, trying to cut off the sniper before he reached the outcrop's end. The other's lead was too great. Before Longarm could close up enough for a certain shot, the man he was chasing rounded the end of the high ledge and disappeared.

For a moment Longarm thought about abandoning his chase, but it was a fleeting idea that he discarded quickly. He kept the livery horse at a gallop, but by the time he'd reached the end of the sandstone formation and rounded it to see mile after mile of broken country stretching ahead he was willing to admit that he'd be wasting time. For mile after mile the terrain in front of him was cut by canyons as well as upthrust jagged pinnacles and columns and high ridges of the red stone that formed the ledge that had marked the beginning of the broken ground.

Longarm's livery horse was panting now, its flanks heaving. He reined in, settled back into the saddle, holstered his rifle, and after another quick glance ahead, fished a cigar out of his pocket. Without taking his eyes off the broken terrain in front of him, he flicked his iron-hard thumbnail over a match-head and puffed the cheroot into a steady coal.

Everywhere he looked there were tower-like formations or long red ridges. No sign of motion was visible, and Longarm needed only that one quick look to realize that a horseman with as much lead time as the fleeing sniper could hide in the maze indefinitely if he had even a little knowledge of the country.

Reluctantly, Longarm turned back. There was no hurry now, and he let the horse set its own pace. He swung to the ground when he reached the car and called, "George? You all right?"

Forbes called back, "I'm doing fine, except my arm's getting sore as a boil. What about that fellow who shot me?"

"He got away in some rough country up to the north,"

Longarm replied, swinging up the sagging steps to the vestibule platform. Forbes was sitting just inside the door. Longarm asked him, "You sure you're in good enough shape to ride back?"

"Of course I am. Just give me a hand getting on my horse, and we can get started."

"Soon as I pick up this cap I dropped when that sniper begun tossing lead at us." Longarm stepped over to the black-and-white checked cap and retrieved it. He tucked it into his hip pocket and went back to Forbes. "Now I'll get you on your feet and down out of the car."

With Longarm's supporting hands to help balance him, Forbes got to the ground and mounted. He handed Longarm his derringer, saying, "This is the kind of gun I ought to be carrying, I guess. Something small that doesn't weigh much."

"It's a good close-range backup gun, but I need more'n it can do in my job," Longarm told him, snapping the chain clasp through the loop on the derringer's barrel and dropping it back into his vest pocket. He mounted his own horse, and they started up the slope out of the hollow.

After they'd ridden a short distance toward Deming, Forbes said, "Well, Longarm, it seems to me that about all we've managed to do today is to find a worthless bunkhouse car that nobody realized was missing and get me shot up."

"Oh, we ain't been wasting time," Longarm replied.

"I hope not, because we don't have any time to waste."

"You mean them high muckety-mucks from the head office are going to pull into town before we get them bonds back?"

"They're due the day after tomorrow," Forbes replied, a worried frown forming on his face. "I was hoping I'd have answers to the questions they'll be asking, but the way things look now, I'm going to be in for a pretty bad time."

"Maybe it won't be as bad as you think."

"I don't see how you can say that. We're no closer to finding that missing suitcase than we were the day it was stolen. And those head-office men aren't going to like that."

"Now, George, just don't go getting all lathered up," Longarm advised. He'd been watching Forbes closely, and he noticed that the Santa Fe man was swaying unsteadily in his saddle.

142

He went on, "I ain't given up yet, and don't intend to."

"I know you've only been here a few days, Longarm, and it certainly isn't your fault that you haven't made more progress, but—"

Forbes stopped suddenly, his face chalk-white. He opened his mouth to try to continue, but before he could speak his eyelids fluttered and he pitched forward over the saddlehorn. Longarm toed his horse closer and reached across to keep the Santa Fe man from tumbling to the ground. Since the end of the fracas at the bunkhouse car he'd been watching Forbes closely. He'd seen other men suddenly keel over as the result of delayed shock following even minor bullet wounds.

For several moments Forbes swayed in a semi-stupor, supported by Longarm's firm grasp. Then his gasping, labored breathing returned to normal and his eyes opened. He lifted himself erect and shook his head.

He said, "I don't know what happened, but all of a sudden I just . . . well, I guess I must've fainted, like an old maid who's seen a mouse run out from under her chair."

"You ain't the first one to feel that way," Longarm assured him. "What we got to do before I can lift another finger on this case is to get you back to town and have that bullet hole cleaned up and a real bandage put on it. But you can quit worrying, George. I ain't outa the woods yet, but I can see the trees starting to thin out. And I'll get back to work on this case just as soon as I turn you over to the doctor."

Chapter 16

After Longarm and Forbes had ridden a short distance, the Santa Fe man said, "I'd almost forgotten in the excitement, but you were going to explain why you set so much store by that old cap we found in the bunkhouse car. Do you feel like satisfying my curiosity now?"

"Sure. You recall when you asked me to tell Buck Tyler that Mr. Carstow'd been killed?"

"Yes, of course."

"Well, while I was in the marshal's office talking to Tyler, that deputy of his, Cal Peters, brought in a hobo that Tyler had told him to kick outa town."

"And Peters hadn't carried out his orders?"

"He hadn't, but there's a little bit more to it than that. You see, Tyler'd taken the hobo to the restaurant there in Deming and fed him a meal, and the old fellow asked him to take him back to see Tyler so he could tell him thanks."

"Tyler never did impress me as being the sort of man who'd buy meals for hoboes," Forbes said, shaking his head. "I'd have thought he'd be more likely to give them a kick instead."

"Funny you should say that," Longarm told him. "That's just what the barkeep at the saloon across from the hotel told me when I mentioned it to him that evening. He said Tyler didn't have no use for hoboes at all."

"Why did he buy dinner for one of them, then?"

"Oh, I asked myself that same question, George," Longarm replied. "And I couldn't come up with no answer why Tyler'd feel like he owed the hobo a meal."

"How did we get off on the subject of the town marshal buying supper for a hobo?" Forbes asked. "What's that got to do with the stolen suitcase?"

"Maybe more than I realized at the time," Longarm replied.

"You're telling me less and less," Forbes protested.

"It'll all come together in a minute, George," Longarm promised. "Now, I didn't see much reason for Tyler treating the hobo to a meal, unless he owed the old fellow something."

"How could he?"

"Well, let me ask you a question for a change," Longarm replied. Forbes opened his mouth to protest, but Longarm silenced him with a headshake and went on, "That suitcase we're looking for ain't the first one that's ever been stolen from your baggage room at the Santa Fe depot, is it?"

"Of course not," Forbes admitted. "It doesn't happen very often, but there are times when the stationmaster has to leave the place for a minute or two. Now and again, some hobo hanging around will—" He stopped short and stared at Longarm. "I see what you're getting at," he went on. "You're suggesting this hobo you're talking about could've slipped in and taken the suitcase?"

"Something like that," Longarm nodded.

"How'd he know which suitcase to take?" Forbes asked. "It wasn't the only one in the baggage room at the time."

"I don't imagine he had any idea he was stealing any more'n just a suitcase that had some clothes he might be able to wear, maybe a few trinkets he could swap for a meal or two."

"Well, that makes sense," Forbes admitted.

"You know, I travel around a good bit in my job," Longarm went on. "I never did see a railroad baggage room that had just one suitcase in it, even in a little place at the end of the line like Deming. I'd imagine there's almost always two or three suitcases somebody's left in the baggage room."

"That's right," Forbes nodded. "They'll check them after they buy a ticket and go over to the Harvey House to eat, or when they come in they'll leave them for the hotel livery to pick up because they don't want to carry them into town."

"So what I figure is that this hobo wasn't after any special suitcase," Longarm said. "He was just looking for whatever he could pick up that he might turn into a few dollars and buy him a drink or two, maybe a meal."

"And he just happened to pick up the suitcase with the bonds in it," Forbes nodded. "You know, that's what the stationmaster suggested in the first place, but Carstow wouldn't listen to him. He was so sure whoever took the case was after the bonds that he wouldn't believe something like that could be accidental."

"I didn't set much store by it being an accident at first," Longarm confessed. "But I didn't know as much then as I've found out since I got here."

"You still haven't told me what makes that cap you picked up out at the bunkhouse car so important, though," Forbes said. "I don't see how it connects up with the missing bonds."

"Oh, that's easy. It connects up through the man I seen wearing it the other day," Longarm told him. "That was when I was in Tyler's office and the deputy come in with that hobo, the one Tyler treated to dinner. The old fellow said his name was Bones Jones, and he had this cap on."

"But he didn't have the suitcase?" Forbes asked. "Because that's what I'm interested in, not what kind of cap he happened to be wearing."

Longarm shook his head. "Tyler and Peters had the suitcase by then. One of 'em likely seen the hobo carrying it down the street and arrested him. Chances are the old fellow hadn't even got around to opening it."

Forbes nodded. "Yes. They'd've had grounds for suspicion, I suppose. Then, when they opened the suitcase at the marshal's office, they found the bonds."

"That's how I figure," Longarm agreed. "They'd know what them bonds were, and I'd imagine they figured they could leave here after a while, soon as things settled down. They'd go to some big town where a bank might not ask too many questions, and then live high on the hog with the money they'd have."

"They weren't far wrong," Forbes said. "The bonds are negotiable. Any bank would take the Treasury bond. They might have had some trouble with the other ones, but the Treasury bond alone would be a good-sized bit of loot."

"Well, the rest of it's real easy to figure out," Longarm went on. "It was too much money for Tyler and Peters to pass up. Tyler told Peters to buy the hobo a meal and get rid of him.

He didn't have any way of knowing the old man would make a fuss about coming back to thank Tyler. And he sure didn't count on me being there when Peters brought him in."

"But how did the hobo's cap get in the bunkhouse car?"

"I figure Peters didn't dare just take him anyplace close to town to kill him," Longarm replied. "He'd've known about that old bunkhouse car. One of the Harvey girls heard them talking about coyotes chewing on bones and burning up bunkhouse cars. That's what they was talking about."

"So Peters killed Bones Jones and left his body in the car," Forbes said.

"How'd his cap get there if that wasn't how it happened?" Longarm asked. "That was likely the only cap he'd have. He sure wouldn't't've just left it there if he was alive."

"It all fits together," Forbes agreed. "But how're you going to prove it?"

"Oh, I'll figure something out," Longarm replied. "All I need is a little time to get some solid evidence together."

During Longarm's explanation they'd ridden steadily, and now the first houses of Deming were just ahead. As they started up the main street, Longarm studied his companion covertly and saw that Forbes's color had returned almost to normal and he was no longer swaying perilously in the saddle.

"I ain't even looked for a doctor's office here," Longarm told him. "I guess there is one in town?"

"His office is right ahead, a few doors past the hotel."

"You figure you can walk to it if we stop and leave the horses at the livery stable?"

"Of course. I'm not dizzy any longer, and even if my arm's as sore as a boil there's nothing wrong with my legs."

"That's what we'll do, then."

Dropping off the horses at the livery stable, Longarm and Forbes walked along the board sidewalk to the narrow little frame building where the doctor's shingle swayed in the mild late-afternoon breeze. There were neither horses nor vehicles at the hitch-rail in front of the office.

"Looks like you won't have to wait," Longarm told Forbes. "And it won't take but a minute to get you fixed up."

Bullet wounds were no novelty to Dr. Jackson. He took one look at the bloodstained bandana on Forbes's arm and asked, "Did the slug go through, or is it still in your arm?"

"It went through," Forbes said.

"Fine," the doctor said. "Come on. We'll go back to my surgery and I'll put some disinfectant on it and a decent bandage and you'll be all right."

While Forbes and the doctor were talking, Longarm had been looking around the bare little reception room. It was barely an arm-span wide, spartanly furnished with two chairs which sat facing the single window that overlooked the street. He asked the doctor, "You won't be needing me back there, I guess?"

"Not unless you just want to watch me fix up your friend," the doctor replied.

"I'd as soon wait out here," Longarm replied.

After the doctor had taken Forbes to the rear of the building, Longarm stood in front of the cramped waiting room and looked out the window. Main Street was almost deserted at that time of the lazy afternoon, and even at a distance he could recognize Cal Peters, the town's deputy marshal, as he approached the doctor's office.

You wasn't far wrong on that guess, old son, he told himself. As Peters drew closer, Longarm could see that he was favoring his left arm, holding it stiffly against his side. He watched the deputy's approach and added to his silent colloquy, *And your aim wasn't as bad as it might've been, because he sure ain't forking that nag like he oughta be.*

Without waiting for the deputy to get any closer, Longarm went through the curtained door into the surgery. Forbes was sitting on a high stool while the doctor wound a bandage around his arm.

"If you're worried about Mr. Forbes, you can stop now," the doctor told Longarm, looking up from the bandage. "He's in good shape."

"I figured you'd fix him up," Longarm replied.

"I'm not dizzy any longer either," Forbes volunteered. "Dr. Jackson gave me a little whiff of smelling salts, and that cleared my head."

148

"That's fine," Longarm nodded. He turned to the doctor, took out his wallet, and showed his badge. "My name's Long, Dr. Jackson. Deputy United States marshal outa the Denver office. I got a little favor to ask of you."

"I always try to cooperate with lawmen," Jackson said. "What's the favor, Marshal?"

"You got a new patient coming in, and I don't want him to see me and Mr. Forbes." Longarm gestured to a door in the wall opposite the entrance to the surgery. "Would that be a back door we can slip out of?"

Though the doctor was obviously surprised to hear Longarm's announcement that a new patient was arriving and puzzled by his request, he answered, "Why, certainly. It opens into my operating room. Just go right through it and you'll see the outside door that'll let you out behind the building."

"Thanks," Longarm said. "Now, if you're finished, we'll make ourselves scarce."

"One more knot in this bandage and Mr. Forbes will be ready to leave," Jackson said, his fingers flicking skillfully as he tied off the bandage. "But if you're expecting trouble, I'd like to know about it."

"I don't look for none," Longarm said. "Just don't say a word about me and Mr. Forbes being here, that's all."

"I don't talk to any of my patients about my other patients," Jackson said a bit stiffly. He patted the bandage and told Forbes, "You'd better stop by in a couple of days and let me take a look at that bullet hole and change the bandage."

"I'll do that," Forbes replied. He stood up and picked up his coat. "I'm ready whenever you are, Longarm."

Longarm led the way into the operating room. Forbes kept walking toward the door, but Longarm put a hand out to stop him. Keeping his voice barely above a whisper he said, "We'll stop here, George. I want to hear what goes on in that surgery."

"Maybe you'd better tell me what this is all about," Forbes said. "I don't—"

"You'll find out soon enough," Longarm replied. "Now just be quiet and listen."

Moving silently on booted feet, Longarm stepped close to the door to the surgery and opened it a crack. In a moment, the voice of the doctor said, "If you'll take your shirt off, I'll see what I can do for you, Mr. Peters. From the condition of your shirt, I can tell that you've lost some blood."

Both Longarm and Forbes inched closer to the door as the voice of Deming's deputy town marshal reached their ears.

"Damn fugitive I was chasing got to me this time, Doc. But, like I told you, it's just a little crease. I made it back into town without any trouble."

"Hazards of your occupation," the doctor said. After a moment of silence he went on, "You're right; it's really too shallow to be called a wound. But you're lucky. Six inches to the right and you wouldn't be here now. All I need to do is paint it up with permanganate and put a bandage on it. Certainly it won't incapacitate you."

"That's fine," Peters said. "Because I've got a lot of work to do before the day's over."

"Fixing you up will only take a few minutes," Dr. Jackson said. "Now, this is likely to sting a little bit. That bullet crease is still pretty fresh."

"Go ahead," Peters said. Then he exclaimed, "Ouch! Damn it, Doc, that does sting!"

"It'll stop bothering you in a few minutes. Hold your arms out of the way now, and I'll get you bandaged up."

In the operating room, Forbes whispered to Longarm, "He's the one who was trying to kill us today! The fellow you shot!"

Longarm nodded and put a forefinger across his lips. Forbes fell silent and Longarm pressed his ear closer to the door, but neither Peters nor the doctor was speaking. After a moment or two, Dr. Jackson broke the silence.

"All right, Mr. Peters. You can put your shirt on now. That wound's not at all bad, but I'd take things easy for a few days if I were you. If it starts bothering you again, stop in and I'll look at it."

"Thanks, Doc," Peters said. "I'll try to—"

Longarm decided it was time for him to move. Drawing his Colt, he pulled the door open and stepped into the surgery. Peters was standing only a step from the door. One of his arms was in a sleeve of his shirt, the other holding the garment. Longarm jammed the cold steel muzzle of his Colt against

Peters's bare ribs before the deputy had time to react to his entrance.

"Just hold still, Peters," Longarm commanded, his voice as hard as the muzzle of the Colt. "You and me have a little business to take care of."

Chapter 17

"Don't kill me, Long!" Peters exclaimed. "I'm not fool enough to try anything with a man like you holding a gun on me!"

"Just keep being smart, then," Longarm told him. He went on, "Doctor, I'll be obliged if you'll do me another favor."

"Name it, Marshal," Dr. Jackson said.

"You're the closest to Peters," Longarm went on. "Take his gun out of his holster and hand it to Forbes."

For the first time the doctor showed surprise. He stared at Longarm and stammered, "I—I'm afraid I don't understand. Mr. Peters is our deputy town marshal."

"Oh, I know who he is, all right," Longarm replied. "But go on and do what I asked you to, if you don't mind."

His brow wrinkled in a puzzled frown, Jackson lifted the revolver from Peters's holster and passed it to Forbes. The Santa Fe man took the Smith & Wesson gingerly and held it clumsily, as will a man unaccustomed to handling weapons.

"What do you want me to do, Longarm?" Forbes asked.

"Just hold on to that gun for minute." Longarm turned to Peters now and said, "Go ahead, get your shirt on. Then me and you are going someplace and have a talk. There's a little bit of unfinished business we got to settle."

His jaw set angrily, Peters finished donning his shirt. He kept his eyes fixed on Longarm while tucking the tail into his trousers, and said when he re-buckled his belt, "I don't know what you mean by unfinished business, Long. From what my boss told me, you and him agreed that you'd stick to what you come here to do for the Santa Fe and stay clear of butting into the way he runs the town."

"So we did," Longarm agreed. "But that was before my case and your town business butted into each other."

"What're you talking about?" Peters scowled.

"Not that you don't already know," Longarm said, "but it won't take long for both of us to find out." He turned his head long enough to ask Forbes, "You feel up to giving me a hand a while longer?"

"I feel fine," Forbes assured him. "And I suppose I'm as interested as you are in getting this thing settled."

"We'll get it all unraveled soon enough," Longarm promised Forbes. "Right now, suppose you go out and get Peters's horse off the hitch-trail and lead it over to the livery stable." He turned back to the doctor. "I'd imagine there's a way for us to get to the livery if we go out your back door?"

"Yes, of course," Jackson nodded. He'd recovered from his surprise by now. "Just walk right on over to it behind the buildings. If you weren't a stranger in town you'd know that Deming doesn't run to back fences."

"I had a hunch that was the way of it," Longarm said. He told Forbes, "Me and Peters will go the back way while you get our horses from the livery. Then the three of us is going to ride out to the railroad yards and hash out a few things."

Peters remained silent as Longarm marched him behind the buildings from the doctor's office to the livery stable. Forbes was waiting with the horses. Longarm jerked his head toward them and Peters mounted his horse in silence. Waiting for Forbes to get on his horse, Longarm mounted.

"I'm going to holster my gun while we're riding out to the Santa Fe yards," he told Peters. His voice hardened as he went on, "Don't get no ideas about making a break for it. You won't be the first prisoner I had to shoot while he was trying to make a getaway."

"I know your reputation, Long," Peters replied. "Like I told you back in the doctor's office, I don't intend to make a fool of myself."

They rode in silence through the fringe of houses that stood between Main Street and the railroad tracks, crossed the main line, and reined in at the office coach on its siding. Peters was docile enough as they entered the car. He slid into the bench seat on one side of the table, and Longarm indicated with a gesture to Forbes to sit on the outside, where he would block any effort the deputy might make to escape. Then he settled into the seat across the table from them.

"Now, then, Peters," he said. "You better be ready to do a lot of talking."

"I haven't got anything to talk about, Long," the deputy replied. A note of bluster crept into his voice as he added, "You've got nothing to hold me on, and all I've heard from you is a lot of talk that don't mean one single solitary thing."

Longarm was not surprised at Peters's reply. Time after time in his career as a lawman he'd seen guilty men change their minds about confessing after they'd been given as much time as Peters had on the way from the doctor's office to the Santa Fe yards.

"Well, now, maybe you're right and maybe you ain't," he told the deputy. "I ain't accusing you or charging you right this minute. I'm just going to lay a few facts out for you to take a look at."

"Go ahead," Peters challenged. "But I'm telling you, it won't get you nothing."

"Well, suppose we see," Longarm went on, his voice guileless. "For openers, I got a witness that says she heard you and your boss talking about some right funny things. Coyotes chewing up bones that's been left out on the desert, and you and him burning up the Santa Fe's bunkhouse cars. You remember that?"

Peters shook his head and said, "Buck and me talks about a lot of things, Long. Who was this witness that told you we said anything like that?"

"Why, one of the Harvey girls. She was waiting on your table when you and Tyler was having supper there the other night and heard you talking."

"You can't expect a man to remember everything he might've said when he was just fanning the breeze at the supper table," Peters protested. "But even if I said anything like that, it was just me and Buck joshing each other, and it don't mean a thing."

"Why, I think it does," Longarm shot back. "Because I was in your office talking to your boss when you brought in an old hobo that called himself Bones Jones."

"Oh, sure, I remember that," Peters said.

Longarm went on, "Now, when you and Tyler was talking

about coyotes chewing on old bones, I got an idea you didn't just mean just any old bones that was laying out on the desert. I figure what you two was really talking about was them coyotes chewing on Bones Jones."

"Why, that's the biggest fool notion I've run into in a month of Sundays, Long!" Peters shot back. He tried to laugh, but only a twisted half-chuckle came from his mouth.

Ignoring the interruption, Longarm continued, "And when you two was talking about burning bunkhouse cars, you didn't mean the ones that's on the sidings at the Santa Fe yards. You meant the one where you'd left Bones Jones's body."

"Now, damn it, Long!" Peters exclaimed. "You was in the marshal's office yourself when you heard the hobo saying Buck gave him a good feed right before I kicked him outa town!"

"I heard what went on," Longarm nodded. "Only I didn't know as much about this case then as I do now. But, be that as it may, I know what I seen and heard."

"And you misunderstood all of it!" Peters almost shouted. He stopped for a moment, then in a quieter voice went on, "All the old man wanted to do was thank Buck for his supper, so I brought him back to the office with me."

"Well, now," Longarm went on. "How many hoboes does the town marshal feed outa his own pocket? And don't answer too quick, because all I got to do is ask at the restaurants how many of them you've brought in for a free meal."

Peters thought for a moment before he replied, "Maybe old Bones Jones was about the only one. Buck fed him because he felt sorry for him. Bones was just an old man down on his luck."

"If your boss was all that sorry, why'd he tell you to kick the old fellow outa town?" Longarm asked quickly.

"Now, you know we can't have hobos bothering these good people in Deming," Peters answered. "And if word got around that they'd get a free feed here, we'd never be rid of 'em!"

"So Bones Jones was a special case," Longarm said. "Your boss didn't pick him out to feed because he was swapping the old fellow a meal for a suitcase?"

"What gives you the idea Bones ever had a suitcase?" Peters snapped back.

"Because there's a suitcase—"

Longarm turned quickly to Forbes and said, "Now, don't you say a word, Mr. Forbes." When Forbes stared at him and started to speak, Longarm added, "I got to remind you that until a judge swears you in on the witness stand in court, you might ruin this whole case by giving away what I got as evidence."

"What in hell's going on here?" Peters blurted. "Nobody knew about that suitcase but—" He stopped short and clenched his jaws as Longarm turned back to face him.

"Nobody knew about that suitcase but you and Marshal Buck Tyler and Bones Jones?" Longarm asked quickly. "Ain't that what you was about to say?"

Peters had recovered quickly from his first surprise. He snapped, "Don't put words in my mouth, Long!"

Longarm paid no attention to Peters's interruption, but pressed on, "You started to say it; all I did was finish it. Bones is dead because you followed Tyler's orders, fed him a good meal so he wouldn't be suspicious, then took him out and killed him. Ain't that right?"

"You've got no proof of that!" Peters protested.

Longarm reached into his hip pocket and produced the black-and-white checkered cap he'd discovered in the bunkhouse car and unfolded it slowly and deliberately. As Peters stared at the cap, his eyes opened wide and a worried frown began to grow on his face.

Longarm said, "I seen Bones Jones when he was wearing this cap, and from the look on your face you remember it, too."

"Well, it looks sorta like the one Bones had on, but I guess if you looked around, you'd find some more just like it," Peters said.

Longarm turned up the cap to expose the label. "Think about it, Peters. This cap was made in England. I'm betting I can convince a jury that there's not another one just like it in all of New Mexico Territory."

Peters opened his mouth to say something, thought better of it, and closed it without speaking.

Longarm went on inexorably, "That ain't the half of it,

either. I know it was you that tried to kill me and him"—he nodded in Forbes's direction without pausing—"out there in that bunkhouse car today."

"I was too far—" Peters started, belatedly realized what he'd been about to say, and stopped short.

Longarm caught him up on his blunder. "You started to say you was too far away for me to see you good." When Peters did not reply, he pressed harder. "You just admitted you was there, even if you didn't come right out with it."

"You can't twist what I didn't say into something else!" Peters protested.

"Oh, there ain't no need to twist anything," Longarm told him. "Me and Forbes both heard you. Now, I'll leave it up to you who a jury's going to believe—both of us, or you."

"All right, Long!" Peters said, defeat in hs voice. "I guess maybe you have got some evidence that'll stand up in court. I'll talk."

"I'm glad you see the sensible thing to do," Longarm told Peters. He stood up. "Come on. There's about enough daylight left for you to take me out to where you buried Bones Jones and the suitcase and dig 'em up."

"Wait a minute," Peters said. "I might as well tell you right off, you won't find that suitcase out there."

"What do you mean?" Forbes asked.

"Tyler took care of the suitcase. I didn't put it in the hole the old man's buried in."

"Where'd Tyler put it, then?" Longarm asked.

"He wouldn't tell me. But if you'll recall, Long, Bones didn't have that suitcase when I brought him into the office while you was there."

"That's right, he didn't," Longarm said to Forbes.

Forbes turned to Peters and said, "I'd advise you not to lie to Marshal Long about that suitcase, Peters. You know, the Santa Fe's got quite a bit of influence in New Mexico Territory."

"Meaning what?" Peters asked.

"You're facing a hanging charge," Forbes reminded him. "If you help us to get our property back, I might be able to get one of the Santa Fe's lawyers to help you when you go to trial. That could make the difference between hanging and just spending a few years in prison."

Peters turned to Longarm and asked, "What about you, Long?"

"You oughta know enough about the law to figure out where I stand," Longarm answered. "I ain't got a bit of use for any lawman that goes bad, but I won't lie to you, Peters. Murder ain't a federal offense. You'll stand trial for killing Jones in a territorial court."

"My offer's the only one you're likely to get, Peters," Forbes said. "You'd better take it while you have a chance."

"Damn it, if I knew where that suitcase is, I'd tell you in a minute," Peters said. "I've gone this far. I sure as hell wouldn't balk at going the rest of the way." He turned from Forbes to face Longarm. "You got to believe me, Long. I don't know where Tyler hid it, and that's a fact."

"I guess I better go talk to Tyler, then," Longarm told Forbes.

"Let's go," the Santa Fe man replied. He stood up and started toward the door of the car, but after he'd taken two or three steps his knees buckled and he was forced to lean on the wall for support.

"You all right?" Longarm asked.

"I—I don't know," Forbes replied. "My legs are weak and I feel dizzy. But I'll be all right."

"I ain't so sure about that," Longarm told him. "Likely you're all give out from what we been doing today, George. You better stay here while I take Peters out to dig up that body. Go over to your car and stretch out."

"I can't leave you to finish this alone," Forbes protested.

"Why not? It's my job," Longarm replied. "Now, you do what I told you to."

"No. I want to go with you when you talk to Tyler," Forbes said. "I'm worried more about that suitcase than I am about the way I feel."

"You sure won't be no help to me if you're wobbly in the knees," Longarm pointed out.

"I'll be all right in a few minutes," Forbes protested.

"And halfway out there you might get took worse'n you are now," Longarm said sternly. "I aim to get this job done before it's too dark to see. Once I start to get a case moving, I like to finish it off just as fast as I can."

"But I want to be with you when you talk to Tyler!" Forbes repeated. "Getting those bonds back is my responsibility, too, you know."

"Sure. I ain't forgot that," Longarm agreed. "I'll tell you what, George. You stay here and get to feeling better, and I'll come by for you when me and Peters gets back, before I go face Tyler."

"Maybe that's the best idea," Forbes agreed. "I suppose I do need a little rest after what's happened to me today. But be sure you come back for me."

"Of course I will," Longarm assured him. He turned to the deputy. "When I get this near to closing a case I get a mite impatient. Let's ride, Peters."

Chapter 18

"I don't see why you've got to make me go dig up old Bones Jones," Peters complained as they left the last houses of Deming behind them.

"You're supposed to be a lawman, Peters," Longarm replied. "So you oughta know the law about proving a case works the same here in New Mexico Territory as it does everyplace else. I don't guess there was anybody seen you kill that poor old hobo?"

"You know damn well there wasn't. I'm not a fool, Long."

"You and me might not be of the same mind about that, but the law says I've got to swear I seen Bones Jones's body and seen how he was killed. And if you happen to change your mind about confessing, I got to prove you killed him. After that, it'll be up to the judge and jury to decide you done it."

"Messing around with a corpse ain't exactly the kind of job a man likes, you know," Peters said.

"Oh, I know that real well," Longarm told him. "But I've run into a few renegade lawmen like you and Tyler before."

"What's that got to do with digging up a body?"

"Any man that's worked on the side of the law's found out a lot of ways to break it, so I've learned it's a good idea to have all the i's dotted and all the t's crossed when I get up in the witness chair to testify against a lawman that's turned bad."

Peters grunted, but made no other response. They rode on in silence with the declining sun in their faces. Longarm was just as glad that his answer had discouraged conversation; in addition to storing landmarks in his memory, he had some planning to do. They'd ridden almost two miles after leaving town before Peters spoke again.

"How much does a federal marshal draw down a month, Long?" he asked.

"Enough to get by on," Longarm replied.

"You got a wife and family to look after, I guess?"

"No. I don't figure a man in my business oughta marry. If I had to worry all the time about leaving some woman a widow, I couldn't put my mind on my job the way I need to."

"Well, be that as it may, I don't figure you'd be drawing down much more than a town marshal gets," Peters went on. "Now, Tyler makes a hundred and ten and I get a hundred. I figure you'd be making about what he does, and that means you got to squeeze every penny just to get by."

"If you've got a mind to try bribing me, you're wasting your breath," Longarm said curtly.

"A man would be what I'd call rich if he split a four-million-dollar haul," Peters said. "I don't guess anybody in our line of work ever gets to see a million dollars all in a pile that he can call his own."

"I told you that you're just blowing in the wind, Peters," Longarm told him, keeping his voice level in spite of his rising anger. "Now shut up! I'm tired of listening!"

Ignoring Longarm's order, Peters went on, "Why don't you think about it, Long? A million dollars!" he repeated. "That'd sure buy a lot of things a man enjoys. Fine clothes, good liquor, rooms in the best hotels, fancy women. You think about it a minute."

"There ain't enough money in the world to tempt me to sell my badge," Longarm said, trying to keep his voice from showing his anger and disgust.

"Don't get sanctimonious," Peters snapped. "You can't tell me you'd turn down a split of four million dollars. There's not a man on this earth that'd turn his back on a cool million."

Longarm realized that there was no way he could keep Peters quiet unless he put a gag on him. He decided to try turning the deputy's talkative streak to his own advantage.

"You've given yourself away," he told Peters.

"How's that?"

"If you don't know where that suitcase is, you wouldn't be talking so free about what's in it."

"Just because I know what's in it don't mean I know where it is, Long. I told you Buck's put it away someplace where me

161

and him can get to it easy."

"If you think he's going to split them four million dollars with you or anybody else, you better think some more."

"What're you getting at, Long?" Peters scowled. "I don't like the way you're talking."

"Well, now, you stop and figure it out yourself. If Tyler had any notion of splitting that money with you, he ought to've told you where he hid it."

"Why, Buck wouldn't pull a trick like that on me!" Peters objected. "Hell, we're partners!"

"How'd you feel about your partner if you got back to town and found out he'd took off with the suitcase?"

"Because I know that old Buck—" Peters stopped short, then he managed a hollow laugh. "You're just trying to stir me up, Long. Now, maybe you better do some thinking yourself."

"Meaning what?"

"Change your mind and throw in with me and Buck. Just don't say no until we get back to town."

"I'll give you credit for trying, Peters," Longarm said. "But I ain't about to change my mind. I'll find the suitcase when I get both of you safe behind bars."

Peters did not reply, and Longarm decided that the renegade deputy had begun to worry about the ideas that their conversation had planted in his mind.

After they'd ridden a bit farther, Longarm decided to continue the softening-up process. He asked, "How come you're talking so free all of a sudden? Back there in town you was tighter-mouthed than a clam."

"You didn't expect me to blab in front of witnesses, did you?" Peters asked. "Out here there's just me and you, and my word's as good as yours on a witness stand."

"I might be inclined to argue that with you," Longarm told him. "Nobody that's fit to sit on a jury's going to let you pull any wool over their eyes."

Peters was silent for a moment. Then he went on, "If this case ever gets to court, that is. You know, all you'd have to do is look the other way while I ride off. I can get back to town and tell Buck we've got to take that suitcase and pull out fast. Then we'd meet you someplace that's safe and split up all that money."

Suddenly revolted by the role he'd set out to play, Longarm decided to make no further efforts to present a false front. His voice was as chilly as an icicle on a sunless morning in December when he replied. "There's one or two things wrong with what you just said, Peters."

"Tell me what they are," Peters suggested. "You've got me and Buck by the short hairs now. If you don't like my idea, come up with a better one of your own."

"I'll tell you what's wrong with your proposition," Longarm replied. "First, I wouldn't turn my back on you, because you're the kind that'd put a bullet into it. Next, you don't know how your crooked partner would take to your proposition. Even if I was fool enough to think about putting in with you two, I wouldn't be a big enough fool to let you walk off with that suitcase. If I took your word that we'd meet someplace and split up, I'd likely be waiting from now till Doomsday for you to show up. But the big thing wrong with your scheme is that I ain't for sale."

"Well, you can't blame me for trying," Peters said.

"Maybe not. But you've tried it and it didn't work, so I don't want to hear any more talk like that. Now, how much farther is it to where you buried Bones Jones?"

"Only a little way. Maybe half a mile." Peters pointed to a rock ridge that rose from the desert ahead and marked the beginning of the rough, broken land beyond. "Just around on the other side of that outcrop."

They rode on in silence to the ridge and around its end. The top of the inverted V-shaped formation was just below the level of their eyes at its highest point. Peters pointed to a heap of large rocks piled up against its face near the center, and Longarm looked for the heap of fresh earth that would mark a grave, but saw none.

"Where's the grave?" he asked.

"Oh, I didn't dig a grave," Peters told him. "He's back of them rocks, in a big crack. I didn't have a shovel, so I put him in that split and piled them rocks over the opening. Figured

163

I'd come back later and dig a grave."

"All right," Longarm nodded. They reached the pile of stones and he reined in and told Peters, "Get on with it."

"You ain't going to lend a hand?" Peters asked.

"Not likely," Longarm said curtly. "Now, get busy."

"I ain't just asking you for fun, Long," Peters said. "That bullet crease you put in my side's beginning to stiffen up. I don't think I can handle those big rocks by myself."

Longarm replied unfeelingly, "You put him in there, so you can get him out. Now stop bellyaching and go to work."

Peters scowled, but dismounted and began removing the stones that closed the fissure. He worked steadily and without any further complaints while removing the smaller stones that blocked the top of the yawning crack. He struggled with the medium-sized boulders that he'd used to chink up the wider opening at the bottom before he straightened up and turned to Longarm.

"That place where you grazed my side's giving me fits," he said. "I can't handle these big rocks here at the bottom by myself, but if you'd feel like giving me a hand, I think I've got this crack open enough so we can reach in and lift him out now without having to move 'em."

"All right," Longarm replied. "It'll save time, and I'd like to get back to town before it gets full dark."

Dismounting, Longarm walked to the fissure and glanced into its shaded depths. Bones Jones's body had been fitted into the gap erect, and had sagged into the shape of an elongated Z, its head and upper torso leaning against one side, hips and thighs bent across the lower section of the narrowing gap, and its knees and feet bent back at the bottom.

No carrion smell came from the corpse; the dry desert air had already begun its slow process of turning the body into a mummy. Though Longarm was sure from the fringe of white hair on the corpse's skull that the dead man had been well into his later years, the skin of his face was already beginning to draw taut and smooth out the wrinkles that creased it.

As Longarm's eyes moved up from the feet to the sagging head while he studied the position of the body he saw the white outline around the exit wound of Peters's bullet where torn cartilage and skin had shrunk and pulled away from the skull and the delicate bones.

Peters had stood by in silence while Longarm studied the body. Now he suggested, "I guess the easiest way to get him out is to lift him up to where the crack's wide enough and then bring him out head-first."

Longarm nodded. "Looks like it," he agreed.

"You're a mite taller than me," Peters went on. "If you'll reach in and lift him and start his shoulders coming out, I'll give you a hand with his belly, and then you can hold him steady long enough for me to grab his legs and bring him the rest of the way outside."

After he'd studied the sagging corpse for a moment, Longarm nodded and replied, "It's as easy a way as any. Let's get on with it, instead of wasting time jawing."

Stepping up to the crevice beside Peters, he leaned forward and slid his hands into the dead man's armpits. The *rigor mortis* that sets in shortly after death had long since run its course, and the corpse was limp and unwieldy. Longarm heaved and slowly lifted the body erect. He stepped back, and Peters bent down to grab the dead hobo's form just below its waist.

Longarm glanced behind him and saw that he could now take a full step backward. As he turned his head to tell Peters to follow him, he saw the flash of steel as Peters pulled a knife from the sheath that was on the dead man's belt and at the same time shoved the full weight of the dead Bones Jones against him.

Longarm let go of the body, brought up his left arm to ward off Peters's downward cut, and pulled his right hand away, grabbing for the butt of his Colt. Impeded as he was by the clumsy burden of the corpse, his draw was much slower than usual.

He moved a split second too late to avoid the quick slash of the blade as Peters brought it down. The knife sliced into Longarm's exposed left forearm, and he felt its painful bite in the few seconds before he freed his Colt from its cross-draw holster and sent a bullet point-blank into Peters's brain.

Thrown back against the stone face by the impact of the heavy .44 slug, Peters's body spread-eagled as it hit the outcrop and hung poised there, arms outflung, the knife dropping from its lifeless hand to fall with a metallic ringing on the rocks that had hidden Bones Jones. Then the dead man's lifeless form slid slowly down the rock-face into a huddle heap.

Longarm stepped back to free his feet from the weight of Bones Jones's body and looked for a moment at Peters, huddled now into a shapeless heap. Holstering his Colt, he turned his eyes from the corpse to study the sleeve of his gray flannel shirt. A red bloodstain was slowly spreading around the edge of the fabric where Peters's knife had slashed it, and the crimson drops were trickling down his hand and dripping from his fingertips.

No wonder that murdering son of a bitch didn't put up much of an argument against coming out here with you, old son, he told himself. *He remembered that frog-stabber on the old man's body and figured if he couldn't talk you into throwing in with him and Tyler, he'd pull a real surprise, cut you down, and get away free and clear. But maybe it's just as well he tried it. Now the territory won't be out anything for a trial, and there's one less renegade lawman walking around preying on decent folks.*

Longarm's wound had begun to throb. He reached into his hip pocket with his right hand before he remembered that he'd used his bandana to bandage Forbes's wound. He stepped over the loose rocks to Peters's body and found an almost-fresh bandana in the turncoat deputy's pocket.

Rolling up his sleeve, Longarm examined the knife slash. The cut was a shallow one, Longarm's lightning reflexes had reacted to the attack in time to keep the knife from cutting deeply. The blade had scored a line across his forearm midway between the wrist and elbow, passed through the skin, and been deflected by the long tendon that protected the brachial vein. The cut had not nicked the vein, but blood was still welling from the ugly wound.

Using his strong yellow teeth and his right hand, Longarm managed to fold the bandana into a strip and wrap it firmly around his arm before tying it off. The tying itself was a long and involved job, and by the time he'd finished his crude bandage the sun had dipped below the horizon and the light was beginning to fail.

For a moment Longarm gazed at the two corpses, decided to risk their discovery by coyotes rather than putting a strain on his wounded arm by trying to load them single-handed onto Peters's horse. He walked over to the horses, picked up the reins of Peters's mount, and tied them to one of the saddle-strings of the livery nag. Then he swung into the saddle and started slowly back toward Deming.

Chapter 19

Although the cloudless sky was still suffused with fading twilight, lamps were gleaming in the windows of Deming's houses by the time Longarm got within sight of the town. His wounded arm was beginning to throb by now, but he ignored the pain. Skirting the edge of town, he rode past the bright windows of the Harvey House and went to the Santa Fe yards.

When he passed the office car in which he was staying, Longarm was tempted to stop for a swallow of Tom Moore and a clean shirt to replace the bloodstained one he was wearing, but he ignored the temptation and went on down the track to the similar car occupied by Forbes. It was also dark, though Forbes's horse, still saddled, was hitched to the rail of the car's vestibule platform. He dismounted and knocked, but Forbes did not come to the door.

Likely he got hungry and went over to the Harvey House to get a bite of supper, Longarm told himself.

Turning away from the office car, Longarm led Peters's horse to the vestibule rail and hitched it beside Forbes's mount. Then he sat down on the step leading up to the platform and lighted one of his long slim cigars. He puffed it slowly and thoughtfully until it had burned down to a stub, then tossed the stub aside and swung into the saddle of the livery nag.

In front of the Harvey House, Longarm dismounted and went inside. Only three or four tables were occupied, and most of the Harvey girls were at the back of the big room making preparations for closing. Nita saw him and came over.

"I was wondering what had happened to you," she said. Then she noticed his blood-soaked shirtsleeve and gasped, "My God! Did you get shot or something?"

"I had a little brush with Peters out on the desert," he replied.

"He nicked me with a knife, but not bad enough to put me outa commission. I had to shoot him, though."

"He's dead, then?"

Longarm nodded and went on, "I'm looking for George Forbes, Nita. Has he been in for supper tonight?"

She shook her head. "I haven't seen him. In fact, I've been wondering what happened to the two of you."

"That's too long a story to tell you right now, Nita. I need to find Forbes without wasting any time."

"You sound worried," she frowned. "Is something wrong?"

"Oh, Forbes took a bullet out on the desert today, and it sorta knocked the props out from under him."

Nita's eyes widened in surprise. "You mean he was wounded in a gunfight?" When Longarm nodded, she went on, "I hope he wasn't hurt badly."

"It wasn't more'n a scratch."

"Was that when you got your wound?"

"No, Forbes got shot earlier, when Peters was trying to kill the two of us."

"Longarm, what on earth has been going on? I haven't heard about any of these things!"

"There ain't been time enough for me to come tell you, Nita," Longarm explained. "I bit off a pretty good-sized chunk today, and I'm still chewing on it."

"Suppose you take time to tell me now," Nita suggested. "I'm working on this case, too, if you've forgotten."

"I ain't forgot. I just been busy. And I can't take the time right now to tell you the whole story. Forbes wanted to go with me when I talk to Buck Tyler about that suitcase with the bonds in it, and I'm heading for the marshal's office right now."

"Are you worried because you think something's happened to Forbes?" she asked.

"Not especially worried, but I need to find him. He made such a much of wanting to go with me when I talk to Tyler that I don't want to leave him behind. I don't guess Tyler's been in here, either?"

"No," Nita frowned. "He ate here at noon, but I haven't seen him this evening. Longarm, have you been to the doctor yet to have your arm looked at?"

"I ain't had time. I just rode in. But, like I told you, all I got was a scratch."

"What happened between you and Peters?" she asked. "Was he involved with that missing suitcase?"

"Him and Tyler both. And Forbes knows now about 'em being mixed up with it. That's what's been bothering me since I found he wasn't in his car."

"Don't you have any idea where he is?"

"Since he ain't here, there's not anyplace else he could be except over at Tyler's office, even if I did tell him to lay low and not go there."

"Is there anything I can do?" Nita asked.

Longarm shook his head. "No. I'm going over and see if I'm right about where he went. Forbes might've got all roiled up and gone to talk to Tyler by himself."

"Please come back and tell me what's going on, Longarm!" she urged. "I've been waiting until I talked to you to wire my daily report to the head office, and Allan Pinkerton's not the world's most patient man with operatives who don't report when they're supposed to."

"I'll be back as soon as I can, Nita," Longarm promised. "If I don't find Forbes pretty quick, both of us might have to go out and look for him."

Leaving the Harvey House, Longarm mounted the livery horse again and rode into town. Deming was just beginning to come back to life after the supper hour. There were lights in the windows of most of the houses visible from Main Street and the street itself was busy.

Saddle horses stood at the hitch-rails in front of the saloons, buggies were tied in front of the few retail stores, and pedestrians were moving along the board sidewalks. Longarm scanned the faces of everyone he passed, but Forbes was not among them. As he neared the end of the street and got within sight of the town marshal's office, he saw that the door was ajar and light streamed from both it and the high-set windows.

A horse stood at the hitch-rail in front of the office. Longarm reined in beside it and dismounted. Tossing the reins over the rail, he went into the office but stopped short after his first step inside.

Buck Tyler sat at the rolltop desk, his swivel chair turned to allow him to face the door. He held a .38 Smith & Wesson in his hand. He raised the weapon and Longarm found himself looking into the round black threatening orifice at the end of the pistol's long barrel.

"Come on inside, Long," Tyler said. His voice was pitched low, at the level of someone carrying on a casual conversation, but its tone was as cold as the steel of the pistol in his hand. He saw the blood on Longarm's sleeve and raised his eyebrows. "I imagine you and Peters must've had a run-in."

"We did. I had to shoot him, even if I'd've rather kept him alive to go to jail with you."

Tyler grinned wolfishly. "For a man with just one good arm who's looking down the muzzle of my gun, you put up a pretty good front, Long. I'll give you credit for that."

"Don't worry about the way I look," Longarm replied. His voice was almost casual as he went on, "I just got a little scratch, Tyler. I can still handle my gun."

Tyler nodded, then said, "We figured it was about time for you to be showing up."

"I'm glad I didn't disappoint you," Longarm replied, his tone still as casual as if he and Tyler had been discussing the weather. "It took me a while to figure out the curves and kinks in this case, but all of it finally came together."

"I was afraid you were going to see the whole thing before we had time to clean up the loose ends," Tyler said.

"You just left too many of them," Longarm told him.

"It's too bad," Tyler nodded, then went on, "I halfway expected you'd figure things out, though. You got to Deming too fast and worked too hard. Of course, that doesn't surprise me, knowing your reputation."

"I guess you mean that as a compliment," Longarm replied. "If it'd come from anybody but you, I'd say thanks. I don't guess you'll mind if I leave off thanking you, though."

"No. As I said, I know your reputation." Tyler raised his voice and said, "You might as well come on out, George.

171

You've been listening long enough to know we're out in the open now."

George Forbes stepped from behind the door, a sawed-off shotgun in his hand.

"I was wondering when you'd show your face, George," Longarm said. "When you wasn't in your car or at the Harvey House, I figured you had to be here with Tyler, so I just moseyed over to tell you I'm ready to close my case."

Forbes stared at Longarm. His mouth was open and his lips working, but no words were coming out. Finally he found his voice, but instead of speaking to Longarm he turned to Tyler and grated angrily, "Damn it, Tyler! I'm sorry I ever got involved in this thing! Now I'm going to have to keep running and dodging the law for the rest of my life!"

"You ought to've thought about that before you let Tyler drag you into the mud with him and Peters," Longarm told him. "And I'll admit, if Peters hadn't slipped up and talked too much, I might not've got to the bottom of your scheme."

"What gave it away?" Tyler asked. "Not that it matters a lot now, but I'm curious."

"Your man Peters give me the last little bit I needed to put all of it together. I'd imagine you told him to see if you could buy me off, didn't you?"

"It would've saved all of us a lot of trouble if he could have," Tyler nodded. "I don't like the idea of being a fugitive any better than George does, but the amount of money involved makes it worth the trouble."

"How did you make Peters confess?" Forbes asked. "He and Buck swore nobody would ever connect me with those bonds."

"Oh, Peters never did call your name, George," Longarm replied. "But when he was trying to get me to throw in with you, he kept talking about how we'd have a million dollars apiece. Them bonds is worth four million, so that just didn't add up. It ought to've been a million and three hundred thousand apiece. That was the first tip I had that if I come into your scheme I'd be the fourth man, not the third. You were the only one that could've been the other man."

Forbes stood silent for a moment, clenching and relaxing

his jaws. Then he turned to Tyler and said, "Well, I guess that settles our scheme."

"Like hell it does!" Tyler snapped. "We're not finished yet, George. Long's the only one that knows about us."

"Wait a minute, now!" Forbes protested. "That sounds like you're talking about murder, and I draw the line there!"

"You ought to've drawn it earlier, George," Longarm said. "I guess you forgot about Bones Jones."

"Tyler and Peters didn't tell me about him," Forbes said. "Not the whole story, anyhow. I knew they'd gotten the suitcase from him, but I didn't know that Peters had murdered the old man until you worked it out and explained it to me."

"That don't make no never-mind," Longarm said. "You're just as guilty of killing him as if you'd been the one that pulled the trigger."

Forbes turned to Tyler and said, "Damn it, you've really gotten me into a mess! What're we going to do now?"

"Why, there's only one thing we can do, George," Tyler replied. "Same as we did to your boss, Carstow." He went on, "Long, step on inside here so George can close that door. The windows are high enough so that nobody can look in from the outside."

Forbes closed the door. Then, in a voice that displayed his growing nervousness, he asked, "What're you planning, Tyler?"

"We've got to get rid of Long, of course," Tyler replied. "He's the only one besides you and me who knows the whole story. Once he's dead, we'll be free and clear, with two million dollars apiece. That ought to be enough to get you over your squeamishness."

"I don't want any further part of this!" Forbes said.

"You don't have much choice, George," Tyler replied. He shifted the muzzle of his revolver in Forbes's direction. "If you're staying with me, close that door and do what I tell you to. It's either that, or I'll have to put you out with Long."

Forbes stared at Tyler for a moment, and Longarm could see that until that moment the Santa Fe man hadn't realized he was at Tyler's mercy and that the town marshal was a relentless killer. He resisted his first impulse to break into their growing argument. Early in his career he'd learned that a falling-out between thieves created opportunities for a man in his situation.

Tyler grated, "Damn it, Forbes, do what I told you to! If we're going to clean up this mess we've got to move fast!"

Reluctance showing in his face and in his hesitant movements, Forbes closed the door and turned the key in the lock.

"That's more like it," Tyler said. "Now, get Long's gun out of his holster. We'll have to wait till the town settles down for the night before we can get rid of him, but he'll be safe enough in one of those cells until we're ready. Then we'll take him out and put him in with Bones Jones. That crack where Peters hid the old fellow's big enough to hold two bodies."

For a moment Longarm thought Forbes was going to obey. But instead, turning back to Longarm, the Santa Fe man stood his ground facing Tyler. He brought up the muzzle of the shotgun and said, "Two killings is enough, Tyler. I can't face any more. You don't need to kill Long. Just lock him up in one of those cells while you dig out that suitcase from wherever you've hidden it, and we'll get away from here. You know the desert. We can be lost in it by the time anybody realizes what's happened."

Behind him Longarm heard a muted rhythmic tapping on the door panel. The rhythm was familiar, but he had not been concentrating on it when it began. He waited, hoping it would be repeated, and almost at once the taps sounded again, a hard tap followed by a soft one, a pair of soft raps, a hard one, then a soft and hard tap. This time he recognized the knocks as being a message in the Morse telegraphy code: $-.\ ..\ -\ .-\ -$ NITA.

Absorbed in their argument, neither Forbes nor Tyler heard the soft, brief taps. Tyler asked, "How far do you think we'd get if we leave Long alive? He'd follow us from now till hell freezes over!"

Longarm eyed the two men. They were staring hotly at one another, their minds filled with the argument that had developed between them. Longarm decided that Tyler was the more dangerous of his two adversaries, and picked him for his target.

Raising his voice, Longarm said, "You better listen to Forbes, Tyler! Another killing's not going to help you a damn bit!"

Behind him a shot rang out and the lock on the door seemed to explode, sending shards of metal crashing into the room. Longarm dropped to the floor the instant he heard the shot, sweeping his Colt out as he went down.

Tyler started to his feet, swinging his pistol to fire at Longarm, but the slug from Longarm's Colt took him in the chest before his finger tightened on the trigger. Tyler got off his shot, but as he triggered the Smith & Wesson he was toppling forward, and the gun dropped from his limp hand. The S&W and Tyler hit the floor at the same time.

Forbes reacted more slowly. He turned as the door burst open and Nita stepped inside. She had her Baby Le Mat in her hand. The little pistol barked and Forbes staggered as the bullet struck him. He stood wavering for a moment, then dropped the shotgun and crumpled slowly to join Tyler on the floor.

"You got here just about the right time, Nita," Longarm said calmly as he rose to his feet. "I was starting to think I might've bit off a mite more'n I could chew."

Chapter 20

"I did a lot of thinking before I tapped out that message to you," Nita said, releasing the sigh that she'd been holding back since she'd sent her signal. "I wasn't even sure that you knew how to read Morse code."

"Oh, I picked up enough of the da-dit stuff to get by with in a pinch right after I started out on this job," Longarm replied. "Except I don't use it often enough to say I know it. But I sure was surprised when it came to me what the taps you made was saying."

"I'd been listening outside the door while you were talking to Tyler and Forbes," she told him.

"You followed me over here from the Harvey House?"

"Not exactly. After you left, I began thinking about what you'd told me, and decided that if you were as close as you said to closing the case, I needed to be on hand."

"So you just up and walked off your job and followed me?" he asked.

"I thought that if you were right I wouldn't need my job as cover any longer," Nita replied. "And if you were wrong, it'd be time for me to come out into the open. So I quit."

"At least you weren't afraid to take a chance."

"Well, it worked this time," she smiled. "I might not be so lucky the next time. But I think I'm just a little bit angry with you, Longarm."

"What on earth for?"

"Why didn't you tell me where you were heading when we were talking a while ago at the Harvey House?" Nita asked.

"Because I wasn't certain-sure until a few minutes ago that George Forbes was mixed up with Tyler and Peters," Longarm told her. "I'd sorta figured he was in the clear after Peters put that slug into him out at that bunkhouse car."

"He covered his tracks very well, all right," Nita agreed. "But we've got one more thing to do before we can close this case. The suitcase with the bonds in it is still missing."

"Oh, I don't imagine we'll have a lot of trouble digging it up. Tyler being the kind of man he was, he'd have put that suitcase someplace where he could keep an eye on it."

"It's probably at his house, then," she suggested. "If he has a house. I don't even know."

"I got a hunch it's a lot closer than that," Longarm told her. "I don't figure Tyler'd have trusted anybody but himself with them bonds."

"You mean it might be right here in his office?"

"If Tyler was like most town marshals I've run into, he'd spend more time here than he would anyplace else."

Nita looked around the little room, and flinched when she saw the bodies of Forbes and Tyler. She turned to Longarm and said, "I don't think my stomach's strong enough to do anything until those bodies are removed. Can't we call in the undertaker before we do anything else?"

"I didn't think about them corpses bothering you, Nita," Longarm apologized. "Just turn your head a minute and I'll pull some blankets outa them cells and cover 'em up."

An iron shackle holding three keys hung on the wall beside the gun rack. Longarm quickly opened the two unused cells and took the blankets off their bunks. He spread the blankets over the bodies and said, "Now look around and see if you don't follow what I been thinking."

Nita had turned her back while Longarm was performing his unpleasant chore. She turned around now and scanned the little office. It was bare except for the bench, the gun rack, and the cells that filled its rear section.

She said, "There isn't a closet or a cabinet or anyplace else where he could have hidden it, and the drawers of that desk aren't big enough to hold a suitcase."

"Look again," Longarm suggested. "You just ain't seeing what you're looking at."

Nita turned and scanned the little room for a second time, and was just turning her eyes back to Longarm when she glanced again at the cell that was being used for storage.

"That cell on the end is the only place it could be," she frowned. "It looks to me like it's used as a storeroom for lost or recovered property."

"I can't think of a better place to put something like them bonds than with a lot of junk that don't seem to be worth a plugged nickel," Longarm told her. He held up the key ring. "It won't take us long to haul that stuff out and take a close look at it."

Unlocking the cell, Longarm and Nita began pulling out the bulging gunny sacks that stood just inside its door. When they pulled out the first sack they saw the muted gleam of leather at the back of the cell, four suitcases neatly stacked which had been hidden by the bags.

"Now, that's something like it," Longarm told Nita. He yanked out the remaining gunny sacks and pushed them to one side. "I bet we'll hit pay dirt in one of them train bags."

Neither of the first two suitcases was locked. They upended them and dumped their contents on the floor, but the bags held nothing except clothing. The third bag was empty; the fourth held more clothing.

Longarm said thoughtfully, "I'd be ready to admit I was wrong if it wasn't for one thing."

"What's that?"

"Why, this empty suitcase. Didn't you get the idea there wasn't nothing but them bonds and some other papers put in that suitcase that was shipped outa the Santa Fe's Chicago office?"

Nita nodded. "Yes. That's all that they reported to us."

"I'd just bet they was sent in the one that's empty now," Longarm told her. "Which means that Tyler's hid 'em someplace else. Now, if you was him, where'd you have hid 'em?"

Nita was looking at the bulging gunny sacks. "The most likely place would be in one of these bags."

"We'll find out real quick if they're there," Longarm told her.

He upended the first sack and emptied it on the floor. It contained a miscellany of clothing, mostly ragged and unfit for further use, three or four mismatched boots, and a couple of crumpled felt hats. Longarm poked at the pile of rags with the toe of his boot for a moment and was about to turn away when he saw the corner of a bulging brown manila envelope sticking out of a heap of clothing. Bending down, he pulled it free.

"Don't hold your breath," he said. "But I think maybe we got 'em."

He slit open the envelope and pulled out a sheaf of folded papers. One glance at the elaborate green scrollwork that formed the margins of one of the papers told him that it was a U.S. Treasury bond. The second had a similar border printed in rich brown; when unfolded it turned out to be the Atlantic & Pacific Railways bonds. The third, embossed in curling script on a heavy parchment-like paper, bore the superscription *Treaty of Understandings and Agreements Between the United States of America and the Republic of Mexico.*

"It's the whole kit and caboodle," Longarm said. "Now as soon as we hand this stuff over to them high muckety-mucks the Santa Fe's sending out here, both of our cases is closed."

"They won't be here until the day after tomorrow," Nita said, her full red lips beginning to curl into a smile. "Since we don't have anything to do until they get here, and I'm not a Harvey girl any longer, I've got a few ideas about how we can spend our time waiting."

"If you're thinking what I am, count me in," Longarm told her. "We'll just lock the door of this place and give the key to whoever's mayor, and let the town clean up here."

In the gray dawnlight that suffused the little bedroom compartment of the office car, Longarm stirred on the narrow bed. He turned on his back and his movement roused Nita. She opened her eyes just as he did and they faced each other with a smile.

"You look mighty good to me this morning," he said. "I got so used to waking up by myself that I forget sometimes how nice it is to have a pretty woman smiling back at me first thing."

"It's a good way to start the day," Nita agreed. She lifted her hand to stroke his cheek.

"I guess I need a shave," Longarm said.

"No. There's something about feeling a man's beard that

gets me all excited and makes me glad I'm a woman."

"I know I'm happy that you are," he replied. "And I feel good having you here in bed with me, too."

Nita's hand moved from Longarm's cheeks to his chest and she ran her fingers lightly through its matted hair. Then she stretched her arm to reach across his chest and touch the bandage that she'd put on the knife cut the night before.

"How's your arm this morning?" she asked.

"I reckon I can put up with it, even if it's a little bit sore and starting to get stiff."

Nita's hand brushed down Longarm's sinewy chest and across the corded muscles of his abdomen and stopped at his crotch.

"You're stiff in the wrong place," she whispered.

"Just keep on doing what you're doing, and I'll be stiff in the right place in about a minute."

"I suppose I can wait that long."

Lifting herself on the elbow of her free arm, Nita bent over and sought Longarm's lips with hers. While they held their long tongue-twining kiss, Longarm felt the warmth of her full soft breasts pressing on his chest. He raised his uninjured right arm and passed his hand across their covering of silken skin, feeling her rosettes as they budded in response to his caresses.

Breathless, they broke their kiss. Longarm pulled Nita up and lifted his head until he could reach the budded rosettes of her breasts with his tongue. She threw her head back and began her catlike purring as his tongue rasped over the pebbled buds, and he felt her hand tightening on his growing erection.

Longarm continued to caress Nita's bulging globes with his lips and tongue until her purrs turned to moans of desire. His erection had grown full now under the urging of her restlessly moving hand, and as she pressed herself to him full-length he could feel the tautness of her body.

"I've waited long enough," Nita whispered. "But I want to be on top this time. You don't mind, do you?"

"Whatever pleasures you pleases me," Longarm told her.

Nita lifted herself above him and knelt to straddle him, and Longarm felt the soft, moist warmth of her ready body engulfing him as she sank down slowly, moaning with little cat cries as she dropped lower and lower on his rigid shaft. She leaned forward and began to roll her hips from side to side, while he continued to divide his attention between the out-thrust tips of her breasts.

Her body began to tremble and Nita stopped the rotation of her hips. She pressed herself down, lifting her torso erect as she rested her full weight on Longarm's hips. Her head was thrown back and her face upturned, her white throat pulsing visibly in the pearly pre-dawn light.

Slowly her trembling subsided, but even after her involuntary movements had stopped she did not move. After she had held her erect position for several minutes, she looked down at Longarm and said, "If I had my way, I'd just stay right here until you made me move. I never have found a man who can satisfy a woman the way you do."

"I'd be the last one even to think about asking you to move, Nita. Fact of the matter is, I feel real good myself."

"Are you ready to feel even better?"

"Why, I'll leave that up to you. Far as I'm concerned, you don't have to be in a hurry to quit anything you enjoy."

"I'll enjoy myself a little while longer, then."

Leaning forward, Nita resumed the measured rotation of her hips. She moved faster as the minutes passed until her body was swaying in rhythm to the shifting of her buttocks and thighs. Longarm lay motionless until Nita's gyrations became a wave of fast jerking spasms. She flung her head back and gasping sobs erupted from the smooth column of her throat.

Longarm realized that Nita had passed the point where she could control her pleasure. He undulated his hips, bringing them up as Nita ground down on him until her body trembled in a final spasm and she cried out and fell forward on his chest.

He held her pressed to him with his uninjured arm as she lay shuddering, until her uncontrollable trembling faded and her sighs died away. After a while Nita raised her head and looked at him.

"I really let go, didn't I?" she smiled. "That hasn't happened to me before."

"All that matters is whether you enjoyed it," he told her.

"Oh, I did! Couldn't you tell that?"

"I figured."

"But you didn't?"

"Not this time."

"But aren't you ready for your own pleasure, Longarm?"

"I can wait till you're rested enough to start again."

"From the way you feel inside me, you're ready now."

Instead of replying, Longarm raised his hips, and Nita's muscles tightened in response to his deeper thrust.

"I guess you really are ready," she said, and began once more to gyrate her hips slowly.

This time Longarm did not hold back. He stayed with Nita until she was once more rocking madly at the edge of control. When he felt her entering her final spasm he let himself join her and jetted as she raised her voice in a wild cry that was half-laugh, half-sob, and fell forward on his chest again, trembling and exhausted.

Nita's sigh broke the long silence that had settled over them. She was still sprawled limply on top of Longarm, and she stirred and rolled away, then propped herself up on one elbow and looked down at his face.

"I'm going to hate leaving you and going back to Chicago, Longarm," she said.

"Nothing lasts forever, Nita," he replied.

"I've learned that. And in our line of work, things last an even shorter time than they might. We'll just enjoy what we've got and say goodbye with a smile."

"You've got a lot of good sense, Nita," Longarm nodded. "And now that you've got that off your chest, you'll feel a lot better when we kiss each other goodbye."

"That won't be until day after tomorrow," she replied. "And I intend to make the most of the time we've got left."

"And so do I," Longarm replied. "And we can start making the most of it again whenever you feel like it."

"I'm going to keep my promise, Longarm, even if I do feel like breaking it," Nita said.

She and Longarm were standing on the platform of the Santa

182

Fe depot. The engineer of the accommodation had already tooted its departure whistle.

"I guess we both feel a little bit like we oughta stay together, Nita," Longarm replied. "But if I've learned anything about you these past couple of days, it's that you don't go back on your word."

"No. Not even if it hurts. I'm going to think of you a lot, I know, and wish things had been different. But if you ever get to Chicago, or I ever get to Denver—"

"Sure," Longarm nodded. "We'll get together again if that ever happens. But them Santa Fe men want me to stay around until they get this deal wound up, and they've already pulled the strings. You saw that wire I got from Billy Vail this morning."

With a final toot and a puff of smoke the train started moving slowly ahead. Nita hurried to get on the steps. She was leaning out, waving, when the train entered the first curve, and he lost sight of her.

Longarm took out a cigar and lighted it. He stood watching the train until a hump in the land hid it from view. Then he walked slowly back to the office car where the officials of the Santa Fe were waiting.

Watch for

LONGARM AND THE STAGECOACH BANDITS

eighty-fourth novel in the bold
LONGARM series from Jove

JAKE LOGAN